15. OCT 12

CU00725150

11

13248

CV	✓	CX	3/6	CY		NA	15/6	NB	✗
NL		NM	3/08	PL		PO		WB	11/04
WM		WN		WO		WS	1/12		

Please return/renew this item by the last date shown.

North
Somerset
COUNCIL

Pirate Pass

Led by vicious cutthroat Morgan DeFete, the Buccaneer Gang plunders the West, kidnapping innocent and fallen women alike and leaving a trail of victims in their wake. They strike terror into the hearts of all who are targeted by them but few are left alive to tell the tale. However, when the gang snatch a railroad magnate's daughter, they go too far.

Manhunter Trace McCoy is a man tormented by the past and in no mood to be chasing down the killers. He has only one mission: to find the outlaw responsible for murdering the love of his life and to kill him.

But within hours of shooting dead his only lead to the killer, McCoy finds himself embroiled in a desperate struggle. Will his gun skills and bravery be enough to overcome the terrible odds which face him?

Pirate Pass

LANCE HOWARD

NORTH SOMERSET COUNCIL	
1 2 0342492 0	
Cypher	15.09.02
W	£10.50

A Black Horse Western

ROBERT HALE · LONDON

© Howard Hopkins 2002
First published in Great Britain 2002

ISBN 0 7090 7080 2

Robert Hale Limited
Clerkenwell House
Clerkenwell Green
London EC1R 0HT

Typeset by Derek Doyle & Associates, Liverpool.
Printed and bound in Great Britain by
Antony Rowe Limited, Wiltshire.

This book is dedicated to Julia Gunderson,
who passed away tragically and suddenly on April 21, 2001.
She will be missed always.

ONE

As a stage clattered around a bend in the snaking trail, Morgan DeFete stared downward, bolts of anticipation sizzling through his veins. Iron tires clanked as they jounced over ruts carved in the sun-baked mud and dust swirled up in great billowing clouds. To Morgan, it sounded like a harp playing in hell.

He sat his horse on a rise overlooking the trail, five men flanking his sides, a motley crew of desperadoes, each nearly as vicious as their leader. For a moment his thoughts slipped back to the days he was known as another man, a man the West now believed dead, vanished into the careless folds of history's fabric. A sigh touched his lips and the images of those days evaporated as quickly as they had come.

For he was now a buccaneer of the Colorado trails and all the West was his ocean.

A laugh drifted from his lips as his attention focused back on the approaching coach. Stands of Douglas fir, Rocky Mountain juniper and Engelmann spruce braced either side of the trail, cutting off any avenue of escape. A musky odor of decaying leaves fragranced the air; the scent pleased him. It was the scent of death.

He swiped his left forearm across his sweat-dappled

7

brow, pushing up the battered felt hat pulled low on his forehead, mindful to turn the hook that substituted for his hand away from his good eye. Stringy black hair stuck out from beneath the Stetson and a week's worth of black stubble peppered his face. An eyepatch covered his left socket. The striking tip of a Blackfoot's knife had plucked out the orb three years back. He'd damn near gone loco after losing that eye, for Morgan DeFete was not a man who tolerated losing in any form. Yet in some perverted way he reckoned he should have been thankful to that now-dead Injun, because it had cast him in the role for which he'd been destined: a marauder, a figure of terror to his men and to his unsuspecting victims.

His gaze traveled to the vicious curving hook where his hand used to be; it glittered in the sunlight, its pitted metal stained brown with the blood of the men who had opposed him. After a botched safe-explosion blasted off his hand, leaving a bloody charred stump, he had forced a sawbones to fix him up with that hook, then driven it through the man's brain.

He shifted, the saddle creaking beneath him, his duster falling away from the cutlass hanging at his left hip. A Smith & Wesson rested in a holster at the right; he reckoned he couldn't be expected to part with everything from his outlaw days. A cartridge-belt criss-crossed his wide chest, and a red sash encircled his waist. Black boots reached nearly to his knees.

His men peered at him, expectant looks on their wind- and sun-beaten faces, unquestioning, knowing well the penalty for interrupting DeFete's reverie before a raid.

'Another hundred feet, matey . . .' His voice came as a harsh whisper and his eye narrowed.

'Reckon it's raidin' time?' asked the man to his left, tugging the slack out of his reins.

'Aye, Higgins, on my order . . .' A blood-haze swept

across his vision and a fever surged through his veins, the fever of the hunt, the kill, the plunder.

The stage drew closer; he could damn near taste the dust in the air. In heartbeats its precious cargo would be his. The day of the pirate was only just dawning and that day would be drenched in blood.

'This the first time you've been out Colorada-way, ma'am?' Jack McBride eyed the young woman sitting across from him in the coach.

She frowned, her face delicate and pale as an Apache peach. With a graceful sweep, she placed a hand to the high ruffled collar of her day dress. 'I declare, Mr McBride, had I known just how savagely stage travel cast lady's internals to jumping all willy-nilly I might never have ventured West.'

With a gusty laugh, Jack McBride plucked a flask from his coat pocket. The older man's face was ruddy, nose bulbous and veined, eyes gray and bloodshot. Dressed in a striped suit with a watch-chain dangling from a vest pocket, he displayed all the earmarks of an itinerant gambler and Violet Chadburn recognized him as such the moment he boarded the stage in Denver. Just the type of scalawag not to be trusted, her father would tell her, but she found him to be a genial sort of fellow who had made the dreadful trip from the train-stop roughly tolerable.

For not the first time since she'd climbed into the coach earlier this morning, she pondered just what had possessed her to become infatuated with the idea of traveling West to visit her father. She supposed a fair amount had to do with the romantic way in which the Mississippi newspapers painted the frontier. Despite her father's resolute declarations that she was too young to be traveling alone she had purchased a train ticket and accorded his predictions of doom to his usual over-protective nature. My goodness, she *was* twenty-one now – practically an old maid! Yet he always treated her like the delicate flower she'd been named after, even more so since her mother's death from pneumonia in '67. Well, he was right: she was delicate in many ways, used to all the advantages and luxuries a railroad magnate such as her father could provide. How he doted over her, smothered her, perhaps, though she knew he only wanted to shield her from the cruel realities of the world beyond her doorstep.

A thin smile touched her pale lips and with hands covered by long suede gloves dotted with eight buttons, she smoothed out the folds of her dress along her lap then tugged down the jacket bodice, unable to deny the feeling of security her father's sheltering provided, while at the same time filling her with a suffocating sensation she loathed.

She was to be wed next June, to a man much like her father, a man who had pleaded with and nearly ordered her not to undertake this journey. She supposed a rebellious streak, a trait her father had passed on much to his distress, demanded she take this time of betrothal to experience for herself the things about which she had only read. The thought beset her mind that the more time she spent on this contrivance the less of a brilliant idea journeying West appeared.

A glance out the window revealed only endless miles of dirt and forest. A film of dust turned her yellow dress to dirty amber. And not a kind word graced her thoughts for the contraption in which she rode. The stage, poorly sprung and minimally cushioned, certainly nothing ever to come out of Concord, afforded no comfort in the slightest to her throbbing tailbone and aching back.

And such indignities! She had discovered the lack of facilities most disconcerting. The drivers had informed her no stage-stand existed between Denver and Danton and Jack McBride had taken endless delight in her predicament the first time the stage had stopped for – how could she phrase it? – *relief.*

In fact, the gambler decreed many of her ways and queries amusing and while much of his conversation created a pleasant distraction, he did seem possessed of a most distressing compulsion to regale her with stories of Indians plucking unsuspecting white women from their coaches and turning them into squaws. A niggling contention in the back of her mind told her she was not entirely convinced he was fabricating the tales. A time or two, she caught herself praying that the coach would somehow magically reach Danton, where her father would be waiting – assuming he received her telegram giving him no choice she was coming. She would not share any of her misgivings with him, of course. She simply could not bear the idea of him telling her she belonged back in Mississippi, attending to the stuffy decorum fancy women held with such lofty affection.

Chin high, she pushed the thoughts from her mind, and peered out through the stage window at the passing forest. The streaking-by woodland only added to the noxious porridge her internals had become.

Another gusty laugh came from Jack McBride and his features grew beatific. 'You'll get used to it after a spell, ma'am. Reckon you delicate types ain't cut out for much travelin' in these parts.'

She raised an eyebrow in exaggerated offense, though she had a sneaking suspicion he was correct. 'Are the trails always this bumpy, Mr McBride?'

He shrugged, uncapping his flask. 'Mostly. Reckon it'll smooth out nearer we come to town.' He held out the tin, offering her a drink of its contents, the odor of which made her nostrils twitch in revulsion.

'I do not partake in spirits, Mr McBride. But thank you

for your courtesy.' Gazing at him from beneath the wide brim of a straw hat with a small crown adorned with ribbon trimmings, she let a thin smile turn her full lips.

'Kinda figured.' He shrugged and downed a deep drink. 'Why you comin' out this way, ma'am? Pardon my bluntness but it's a right dangerous place for your type.'

She arched an eyebrow. 'My type, Mr McBride?'

'No offense, ma'am. Only meant it's a long way from home for a fine lady such as yourself.'

She laughed that delicate little laugh she'd spent years perfecting. 'I suppose you are right, Mr McBride. My father was born out West, came East and met my mother, then attained his fortune in the railroad industry.'

A surprised look crossed the gambler's face. 'You're Rutherford Chadburn's daughter, the railroad man?'

She nodded. 'Why, yes, Mr McBride. That is why I have come here, to see him.'

'Ain't the only reason, I reckon.'

'How is that, sir?'

'You want to show your daddy you got gumption, that the sun and moon don't set by his orders. That thinkin' always leads to trouble, though.'

'You are most perceptive, Mr McBride.'

He let out a bellowing laugh. 'Hell, that were true I'd be a rich man today!'

'Gambling is the Devil's wages, sir.'

'And winnin's the Lord's bounty, I figure.' He grinned and she smiled a warm smile.

Her tone turned serious. 'What do you mean, it leads to trouble, Mr McBride?'

'Well, just like I said about Injuns takin' white squaws and such. West's got some rough types, too, men just lookin' for somethin' pure to sully. Don't want to see nothin' happen to you.'

The smile came back to her lips. 'I thank you for your

concern over my honor, Mr McBride, but it is hardly necessary.'

He beamed. 'Why, ma'am, you make an old man pleased as a flea with his own dog.'

She giggled, some of her tension dissipating. 'And what of you, Mr McBride? Why do you travel to Danton?'

He shrugged, swallowed another gulp from his flask. 'Reckon it's because I got nowhere better to go. Been on the move ever since Hildi passed on and don't reckon I want to stop long enough to think about her.'

Compassion rose in her bosom. 'How sad, Mr McBride.' Her voice came low, comforting. Here she was looking forward to her life, marrying in early summer and he was drifting, alone, with little more than the clothes on his back, a flask of whiskey and an empty heart. Times like these she realized the advantages she had were more than she deserved.

A shot blasted from beyond the coach, filling the day with thunder. Lead punched through one side of the stage, passing only inches before her startled face, and continued out the other. The gambler started and the flask jumped from his grip, contents splashing across the pleated draperies of her dress.

The vehicle took a bounce that threw her backwards against the rear panel. Breath exploded from her lungs and she let out a small bleat.

'What the hell—' blurted McBride, endeavoring to grab his flask from the floor and save some of the contents from spilling out. 'Powerful sorry 'bout your dress, ma'am.'

She caught her breath and felt her heart start hammering against her ribs. Face washing white, she gazed at him with fear-widened eyes. 'That was a gunshot, was it not, Mr McBride?' Her voice trembled and she clutched at her parasol, a foolish thought flashing in her mind it would stop a bullet.

The gambler gave a jerky nod, as though he had forgotten about the bullet in his effort to save his liquor.

'Hell, yer right!' His voice jumped in pitch and he capped the flask, tucking it into a pocket.

The stage swayed, rocking side to side in a sickening motion that threatened to bring up her stomach. She clutched at her belly, dropping the parasol.

'Why would someone shoot at us, Mr McBride?' Her voice wavered, on the verge of climbing to the shrill pitch it favored whenever she bordered on hysterics.

Sweat sprang out on the older man's forehead. 'Bandits, likely.'

'We are carrying no money, Mr McBride, nothing of value. What possible interest could robbers have in us?'

He shrugged. 'Reckon I don't rightly know, 'less they want somethin' else, or maybe they're Injuns.'

The thought of being made into a white squaw flashed through her mind and she nearly broke into tears. She was foolish to think she could survive on her own in such a hostile environment. Nothing about the West appeared romantic in the least any longer. The entire vista was all just threatening and alien and she should never have defied her father's wishes.

A series of shots rang out and with each she jolted in terror. An agonized screech came from the front and one of the drivers was suddenly hanging from the side of the coach, his foot entangled in something she could not see, his face a deathmask. His body slammed against the carriage with each bump.

Violet screamed; she could not hold it back. Fear exploded in her being and she had no chance to stop it from bursting forth. She felt somehow foolish afterward, but too stricken to even contemplate apologizing for her loss of control.

Teary-eyed, she peered at Jack McBride. The scream

must have rattled the gambler sufficiently because he was suddenly blubbering and clutching with bleached hands to the sides of the coach.

The stage slowed as further shots punctuated the remaining driver's shouts to bring the neighing horses to a halt. The dead man dangling over the side jerked loose and went tumbling over the ground.

Unable to hold them back any longer, she let tears stream from her eyes at the sheer brutality of the act. She had never witnessed a killing and it was a sight that would haunt her until her dying day.

The stage clattered to a stop. Another shot rang out and a heavy thump from the front told her the second driver had been murdered.

For a suspended moment everything went still. She heard the horses snort, then men shout and whoop and she bit at her lower lip.

She was going to die. She had little doubt of it and the realization terrified her beyond words. Nothing on the stage held any interest for a robber and when they discovered that fact they would turn their attention to its passengers. While her father had always been there to shelter and protect her, this time he could not. She was alone and vulnerable, more so than she ever believed possible.

The thoughts must have mirrored on her face because McBride reached out and clutched her hand, squeezing her fingers in a fatherly gesture, though obviously terrified himself. She peered at him and he tried a feeble smile to reassure her, but it didn't work and a sob escaped her lips.

A panicked thought forced its way into her mind: What if they didn't merely kill her? What if they . . . left her soiled? Perhaps death was preferable to the disgrace and guilt that would follow the forced surrender of her maidenhood.

Jack McBride squeezed her hand tighter. 'Don't you

worry none, ma'am, you'll be all right. Don't you worry.' His voice held no confidence and his words were empty. No, she would not be all right. Even if she got out alive nothing would ever be the same. Fear would be her constant companion, and if they took her purity the shame that would plague her mind would make her wish they had taken her life.

'Get out of the coach!' A voice snapped like another gunshot and she jolted, looking to McBride for guidance.

He frowned, the fear in his own eyes reflected like twin skulls. 'We best do what they say, ma'am. Maybe things won't be so bad.'

'Do you honestly believe that, Mr McBride?' Tears choked her voice.

A prolonged sigh escaped his lips. 'No, reckon I don't, but we got no choice in the matter.'

McBride gripped the door-handle, stepping out first. She stumbled out behind him, retrieving her parasol and clutching it for comfort but finding none.

Six men on horseback flanked the stage in a semicircle, each holding a rifle except for the lead bandit. She caught herself glancing at the driver's seat against her better judgment and spotted the driver slumped there, a spray of crimson splattering the stage behind him.

She gasped, letting out a small bleat.

'What's a-matter, missy?' asked the leader. 'No belly for death?'

She gazed at the man, whose face sent a jolt of terror through her. Stubble darkened his jaw and an eyepatch covered his left eye. His one dark orb, roving, held only cruelty and hate, no mercy, nothing even remotely human as far as she could see. In place of his left hand was a hook, the reins looped around its vicious curve.

'Why have you stopped us, sir?' McBride's query came hesitant, shaky. 'This is a passenger stage. We have no gold, nothing of value for a man such as yourself.'

The leader let out a shuddering laugh that made her legs go weak. 'You got far more than gold aboard your vessel, matey.' He unwound the reins from his hook and dismounted. His duster swept aside and she glimpsed a sword hanging at his hip. As the man stepped towards McBride, her heart pounded so hard she could barely breathe.

Stopping before McBride, the bandit's lips lined into a hard expression. 'Aye, you got a far more valuable treasure, matey.' His gaze flicked to her and Violet let out a strangled sound.

'Christamighty, no . . .' McBride mumbled. 'She ain't done nothin' to you.'

The man uttered a roaring laugh. 'She didn't have to, sir.' His hand swept to the cutlass at his waist, pulling it free with a prolonged *shrik* that sent a chill shuddering down her spine. Her eyes widened in utter horror as the sword flashed up, blade streaking with sunlight and silver as the bandit thrust it clean through the older man's body. McBride's face froze in a mask of agony and terror. The blade embedded itself into the stage, leaving the gambler suspended, blood bubbling from his quivering lips.

With a powerful tug, the leader withdrew the blade and McBride slumped to the ground, back propped against an iron tire.

The bandit squatted, wiping the blood from the blade on the gambler's trousers. Crimson welled across McBride's vest.

The leader peered at the dying man, dark eye intense and damning. 'You live long enough for anyone to find ya you tell 'em somethin' for me. Tell 'em pirates have a new ocean to sail, an ocean of mesquite and dust and all its ports to plunder. This is only the beginning of the Buccaneers' reign of blood.'

McBride's eyes turned glassy. Words came out in a broken bubbly voice.

'Who . . . are you?'

The leader stood and thrust the sword back into its scabbard. 'Morgan DeFete at your service, sir.' He gave an exaggerated bow.

The old man's eyes glazed and she knew he would tell no one what had happened here today. The third death she had witnessed in a handful of moments, it proved too much for her frail composure. Shock crushed her, suddenly and completely, and she crumpled, blackness swirling in from the corners of her mind.

A voice boomed above her and through blurry vision she saw the leader bending over her, leering, his good hand groping her breast. 'Hell, you city women ain't made of too goddamn solid stuff, are ya?' His laugh mocked her, but she suddenly didn't care. She let the blackness guide her into merciful unconsciousness.

TWO

Trace McCoy sat at the end of the bar in the Sonofabitch Saloon, a whiskey in one hand, a domino in the other. On the counter next to his hat lay a blue velvet pouch, the one *she* had sewn for him those many years ago. Seven tiles lay spread in a line before him, pairs with like numbers separated into a pile to the left. The dominoes, carved from bone, were double six and arranged for a game of solitaire he had concocted to distract himself when thoughts of the past haunted his mind. He set the bone, a four, beneath a five, but it proved to be his final move. He had lost. Again.

The way he had lost her. The way he had lost any chance at a normal life.

Karen had given him the set as a gift for his twenty-first birthday. Although she had been gone five years now, he recollected the day as clearly as if he had lived it moments ago. He s'posed he couldn't say he carried them for luck because he rightly hadn't had any and if his record at beating himself at solitaire were any indication he never would. He kept them more for sentimental reasons, though no one would have accused him of being a sentimental man, at least not any more.

He lifted his glass to his lips and swallowed a deep drink. It provided him no comfort; it never did, but he sought solace in the whiskey all the same. A whispered laugh came from his lips. Nothing would soothe the ache of vengeance burning in his soul; nothing except the death of the man responsible for Karen's murder. And at long last he had discovered a lead to that man, a spark of hope.

That lead sat at the other end of the bar, hunched over a glass of redeye, looking as if the world owed him every goddamn thing on a silver platter and the sins of the past would never come a-calling.

He was wrong, dead wrong. Those sins *would* come a-calling and they would come in a blast of hellfire from the end of the Peacemaker at Trace's hip. Enough grease coated the tooled-leather holster's interior to allow the six-shooter to slide out as slick as a card from a tinhorn's sleeve and its filed-down sight would prevent any chance of a snag. Long hours of practice had honed his skills with the piece to a razor-edge.

The angry spirit raging within impelled him to shove the barrel into that hardcase's mouth and pull the trigger now. His hand itched to go for the Colt, deliver punishment to the loathsome sonofabitch who had participated in Karen's death that day so long ago. But a moment's satisfaction would destroy his only prospect of finding her killer.

The man didn't recognize him, that was plain. Perhaps the hardcase had murdered so many their faces blurred into a blank canvas of stifled screams.

Without lifting his head, the outlaw grunted at the barkeep for a refill. Trace sat just close enough to overhear anything the man said in a raised voice. The hardcase was well into his cups and anything that came out of his mouth came out with volume.

The outlaw glanced his way, dark eyes locking with Trace's bitter blue ones. For a heartbeat Trace thought it was over, that the man had caught the vengeance glittering in his gaze and was going to do something about it.

No . . . not yet . . .

The hardcase turned away, and Trace breathed a sigh of relief. He'd been following the man for over a week, after a chance encounter in a barroom led to the discovery that at least part of the old Harrigan gang still lived. Trace recognized the 'case instantly, in fact would recognize any one of the outlaws as if he'd laid eyes on them yesterday. In his mind it *was* yesterday. It would always be, as long as a sonofabitch named John Harrigan walked the earth. As long as her death went unpunished, unavenged.

Unforgotten.

The man's movements had struck Trace as peculiar. Wandering from town to town, he spent most of his time coddling hangovers, but Trace wondered whether the man had some sort of method to his peregrine activity. The hardcase almost appeared to be searching for something, or someone.

Only a handful of patrons occupied the saloon, engaged in games of chance, primarily poker. Cheroot-smoke swirled in the dusky shafts of sunlight arcing through the grime-coated windows. Two bargirls served drinks and leaned over players' shoulders, hoping for a score. They weren't the only ones, though Trace's score would be a hell of a lot more bloody.

Five men and their leader that day. Were they all still alive? Still with Harrigan? Or was this man the sole survivor? Nothing had been heard of the gang for the past two years and that had riddled Trace with doubt and worry. Until last week he'd begun to think he would never track down the bandit. While he'd encountered no first-hand reports of the outlaw being killed, some speculated he had simply vanished, either done in by Indians or perished of plain orneriness. He'd become inclined to believe those rumors, though he never stopped hoping for a clue to the man's true fate. An easy death wouldn't do. Not for a hardcase the likes of John Harrigan. A man like that deserved to suffer, to know true fear, the same fear he left frozen in the eyes of his victims. To be robbed of that by some act of nature or Western mishap would have stripped Trace of any chance at accepting her death, of casting off even a fraction of the hate he carried day in and day out for outlaws and their kind, and for himself.

His hand went to the scar running along the underside of his chin, a reminder of where Harrigan's stone opened a gaping cut, and a flash of memory tortured his mind. He saw her face, her beauty, the blood streaming from her forehead and heard her screams echo from the depths of his despair.

Christamighty.

His hand trembled as he took it away from his chin and sweat beaded on his brow. He fought the blood-red images away. It wouldn't do him a lick of good to dwell on that now, but it served to remind him he was just a man, not a machine of vengeance, and a damned unstable one at that.

Fingers drifting over the dominoes, he turned them face down and mixed them up. Selecting seven, he placed them in a row, turning the rest face up. Another game; another chance to know the the time of sweet retribution had finally arrived.

A sound caught his attention and he looked up to see a man stepping through the batwings. The fellow paused just inside the doors and glanced about, as if searching for someone. His gaze lingered on Trace then shifted to the hardcase and finally the 'keep. Trace sized him up. A short, wiry man, the sort who likely possessed a raw strength and force of will in his younger days. He carried himself with a sense of leadership and presence that belied the stoop in his shoulders. His hands appeared used to labor, though he wore a suit that had likely cost more than Trace's saddle. Plucking a derby hat from his head, he smoothed out thinning strands of iron-streaked hair. The man's eyes held a painful intensity and he exuded an air of – what? Sadness, laced with worry. It looked out of place on the fellow but it was there, plain as day. He had lost something, something precious to him, and wanted it back. Trace recognized the look; it was one he saw staring back at him whenever he gazed into the mirror.

The man threaded his way through tables. Stepping up to the bar, he placed his hat on the counter-top.

'What's your poison, gent?' The 'keep's tone was that of a man who had asked the same question a thousand times before and no longer gave a damn.

Trace barely caught the man's answer. The sadness on his face seemed suddenly more intense as he reached into his pocket, laying a tintype on the counter-top.

'I am not here for whiskey, but I will pay you for information.'

The bartender arched an eyebrow. 'What kind of information?'

'I am looking for this girl.' He tapped the tintype.

The 'keep glanced at the likeness and shook his head. 'Sorry fella, can't help you. Ain't the type of gal we get in here. Who is she?'

The man's face fell. 'She's my daughter. My name's Rutherford Chadburn.'

Surprise crossed the barman's features. 'The railroad guy?'

The older man nodded. 'My daughter is missing. I am searching for her.'

The 'keep leaned against the counter. 'Why didn't you hire detectives to find her?'

'I don't want detectives, not with who is responsible. I am looking for one man. A bounty hunter.'

The words must have penetrated the hardcase's stupor because his head jerked up and his eyes narrowed. He stared at the railroad man with an irritated glare.

Trace had heard of Rutherford Chadburn; likely damn few in Colorado hadn't. The man had made big news with the track his company was laying throughout the territory. But that recognition went deeper with the hardcase, it was plain to see.

'You got a particular bounty hunter in mind?' the barkeep asked.

Chadburn's gaze dropped, came back up. The hardcase's eyes grew bitterly intense. 'His name's Trace McCoy. I hear tell he's ruthless.'

You heard right . . .

Trace's belly tightened. The last thing he needed was anyone looking to hire him right now; he had personal business waiting on him, business that had gnawed out his innards for five long years.

The bartender's eyes cut to him and Trace gave a slight shake of his head, but the railroad man caught the unspoken exchange and started to rise.

The hardcase, too drunk or too preoccupied with his own schemes, missed the signals. He clamped a hand on the railroad man's wrist. 'Who the hell you say you were?' His tone came challenging, words slurred.

'Unhand me, sir.' The older man tried to pull his arm free but the hardcase held fast.

'You best be thinkin' about goin' back where you came from and forgettin' 'bout lookin' for your daughter, friend.'

Chadburn's eyes flamed. 'Take your hand off me. I won't tell you again . . .'

A sense of command rode the man's voice and Trace

reckoned even at his age Chadburn might have had the gumption to back up the order if it weren't for the fact the hardcase had suddenly drawn his gun and jammed it against the man's temple.

The railroad man's face paled. He realized he had stepped into something unexpected and probably had no idea why. Trace had no notion, either, but right now he didn't care. Anger blazed in his veins and the memory of that day flashed in his mind. Something deep inside took control then, something dark, something remorseless. His hand swept toward his Peacemaker, bringing the weapon up even as he came off of his stool.

The notion must have penetrated the hardcase's mind that a new and greater danger had suddenly presented itself, because deadly realization crashed over his cruel features.

Had things occurred at a slower pace Trace might have gained enough time to talk himself out of killing the only lead he'd encountered in five years. But they didn't. They happened with blinding swiftness and hair-trigger reflex.

His Peacemaker came level even as the hardcase's gun swung from the railroad man's temple towards Trace.

Not in time.

The barkeep jumped back and Chadburn twisted on his stool, leaning left, gaze locked on Trace.

Flame erupted from the Peacemaker's muzzle. The thunder of the shot reverberated through the barroom and roared in his ears.

Shock and fear froze in a deathmask on the hardcase's face. His finger spasmed, triggering a shot. The recoil kicked the gun from the man's nerveless grip; it skidded across the floor. The bullet buried itself in the bartop.

A bargirl screamed behind Trace.

The hardcase stumbled backwards, a starburst of crimson exploding across his chest. He slammed into the bar then rebounded to the floor, throwing up a cloud of sawdust.

Trace stared at the man, frozen, knowing full well he was dead and any chance of following him to John Harrigan had died with him. He slid the Peacemaker into its holster and collapsed on to his stool. He gulped down the rest of his whiskey and stared at the empty glass, fighting a wave of utter hopelessness and despair. How would he find Harrigan now? Would another five years pass without a lead? Another five years carrying the burning grief in his heart and the blistering thirst for vengeance in his soul?

'Goddammit . . .' he muttered, voice bitter and low.

The barkeep's face looked a shade paler. 'Christ on a crutch, I ain't never seen death happen so fast.'

Trace glanced at him, finding the statement a foolish indictment of his skills. That hardcase was lucky, too damned lucky; he had died instantly. It was far more than he deserved.

The barman pointed to one of his girls. 'Go fetch the marshal.' She nodded and hurried for the batwings. 'Don't you worry none, Trace. It was self-defense pretty as you please.'

'I ain't worried . . .' His voice came barely audible. 'The bastard deserved to die, just not so easy.'

The 'keep nodded, backing away. As though in shock, Rutherford Chadburn hadn't moved, but now some of the color began to bleed back into his face. He stood, taking his tintype from the counter, and walked over to Trace, indicating the next stool.

'Mind?' Chadburn's voice came remarkably steady for a man close to dying a moment before.

Trace glanced at him. 'Would you leave me be if I said yes?'

The railroad man appeared taken aback but wasn't

about to be swayed. He pulled out the stool and sat. Trace grunted and began setting dominoes upright, about an inch apart, in no mood to discuss business.

The older man's gaze settled on him. 'I came here looking to hire you, Mr McCoy. I've searched through every saloon from here to Denver to find you.'

'I ain't for hire.'

Confusion played on the railroad man's features. 'But I understood you went after men who were guilty of—'

'You understood wrong, least at this point.'

'Please, Mr McCoy . . .' He placed the tintype on the counter before Trace. Trace gazed at it. She was a pretty, delicate kind of girl, and for an instant something pulled at his compassion, the man he once was.

'Like I said, I ain't interested.' He went back to setting up the dominoes.

'You don't understand, Mr McCoy. I am a proud man but I will beg if I have to. My daughter means everything to me. She was abducted by a gang who killed two drivers and a gambler riding the stage with her. I have no idea why they wanted her or if she's even . . .'

'It's your fault that man's dead.' The words came bitter and blaming and Trace wasn't in control of his humanity enough to give a damn.

A startled expression hit Chadburn's face. 'W-what? What do you mean it's my fault? I don't know why that man accosted me.'

'No?' Trace glanced up at him, judging the man was telling the truth, but the fact provided him little incentive to change his pronouncement. While it did pique some small part of his manhunter's curiosity as to why a member of Harrigan's gang would suddenly decide to go loco on a railroad man searching for his daughter, he had more important things with which to torture himself.

The railroad man shook his head. 'I never laid eyes on him before.'

'That man's a hardcase, wanted for murder and robbery. I been trackin' him a week, Mr Chadburn. I needed him alive. Weren't for you, he would be.'

'I'm afraid I don't understand. I came here hoping to hire you to find my daughter. I asked for no trouble from that man.'

A humorless laugh escaped Trace's lips. 'He sure as hell gave it to you. You hadn't come in here I wouldn't have been forced to kill him.' It struck him as petty, putting the blame on the railroad man when in fact it belonged with the dead outlaw, but rationality wasn't his strong suit when he started feeling sorry for himself.

'I would apologize, Mr McCoy, if I had any notion what it was I was sorry for. I meant no harm to anyone. I am just at my wits' end and would do anything to get my daughter back alive.'

Trace saw the pain in the man's eyes strengthen; it stared back at him like a blood-stained reflection of his own soul.

You're a bastard . . .

'That man was a domino, Mr Chadburn.'

The older man sighed. 'You've lost me, I'm afraid.'

Trace flicked out a finger, knocking the lead domino over until it slammed into the next and the rest in turn. The row toppled with hollow clacks. 'I been followin' him, hopin' he would lead me to someone. When he fell I wanted it set up so that someone would fall with him, along with the rest of the gang responsible for—' He caught himself. That was none of the railroad man's business. A man like Trace McCoy hoarded his pain; he did not share it.

'Responsible for what, Mr McCoy?' Chadburn's eyes narrowed, peering at him as if searching for some open doorway in Trace's soul. But all doors were locked and that's the way they would stay.

'Let's just say he's responsible for me losing at solitaire again.'

Rutherford Chadburn leaned forward, fingers tracing the features of the girl in the tintype. When he looked up again, Trace felt compassion struggle to assert itself but forced it away. He was in a goddamn bitter mood and preferred to stay that way.

'I got no idea why you're looking for whomever it is you are, Mr McCoy, and I can't force you to tell me. A man's got a right to his secrets. I can't force you to look for my daughter, either. I can pay you, whatever you want, in fact, but if you don't do this for me I will find that gang myself, somehow.'

'What then, Mr Chadburn?' Trace asked it in all sincerity and the older man stared at the counter for long moments.

'I want them dead. I'll make no secret of that. That is the reason I wanted you instead of the law. But if that's not possible I'll pay them whatever it takes to have my daughter back and swear in any goddamn court they aren't responsible. That might not make sense to a fella like you but at the very least it should tell you how desperate I am.'

Trace wondered if the uncomfortable feeling gnawing at his innards was his conscience stirring. 'I got me a case to work on, Mr Chadburn. One I been workin' on a long spell now. Got no time for nothin' else.'

A tremble worked its way into the railroad man's hands as he ran his fingers along the edge of the tintype. 'You ever lost someone, Mr McCoy? Someone you loved more than life itself?' Chadburn drew the tintype towards him, gazed at his daughter, then tucked it into his pocket and stood. 'I'll be at the hotel until I can figure out some way to find those men.'

Trace's eyebrow arched. 'What chance you expect to have against this gang even if you do find them? You really think they'll just let you pay them and walk away with your daughter?'

The railroad man shook his head. The look in his eyes said he didn't believe that but was willing to commit what amounted to certain suicide over it all the same. 'What choice do I have, Mr McCoy? I'd walk into Hell itself to have Violet back.'

'You just might have to . . .' Trace began flipping the dominoes over again. He could no longer make himself look into the man's eyes. Sometimes a body just had to be content with being a sonofabitch.

The railroad man took his hat from the bartop and walked from the saloon as if the weight of a thousand anvils were resting on his shoulders. After Chadburn left, Trace's head rose and he breathed a long sigh.

'Yes, Mr Chadburn, I know damn well what it feels like to lose someone who means more than life itself.' His words drifted out, stained with guilt.

The 'keep came over and poured Trace another glass, eyed him with a frown. 'Why didn't you help that man, Mr McCoy? Ain't none of my business, but from the way he looked he really loves his daughter.'

'You're right, it ain't none of your business.' Trace downed the whiskey then scooped up the dominoes and dumped them into the velvet bag. He rose, shoving the pouch into his pocket and grabbing his hat. He felt in no mood to debate his decision, especially when the 'keep likely held the moral edge.

'Tell the marshal I'll be in my room at the boarding-house till dawn if he wants me. After that he ain't likely to get a statement.'

The 'keep nodded. Trace walked over to the dead man and peered at the sprawled form. A burst of unbridled anger surging over him, he kicked the man in the ribs then headed out through the batwings.

At a quarter to eight the Danton saloon held only a handful of patrons and Coralie Duvalier sighed at the lack of prospects. If the barroom didn't fill up soon she wasn't going to make enough money tonight to pay the owner his more than generous share. He was like to try beatin' the hell out of her again if that were the case. At the thought of his rough fists pounding into the soft flesh of her belly nausea burned in her throat and heat surged through her cheeks. Her gaze flicked to the blocky man behind the counter wiping out a glass, then away.

Christ, she hated this life, hated being what she was and doing what she did, but what else was there for a woman like her? Her mama never had given a damn about her little girl's welfare or breeding and her pa, bless his departed soul, died when Coralie was four. She grew up far faster than a woman was supposed to, especially after some of her ma's beaux got their hands on her. From there she couldn't even recollect the number of saloons and cathouses in which she'd worked. Too many for a gal of twenty-five, truth be told.

Things hadn't gotten any better since she'd come to Danton, either. She wondered how she had deluded herself into thinking they would ever change. Maybe the notion her life would improve was what kept her goin', tolerating the dung- and sweat-stinking men who bought her services. She wished she could blame those men, hate them, but knew the fault lay with her and many a time during the blackest part of the Western night she despised herself, prayed to a God who likely paid no attention to whores for an end. That end never came. Now she felt trapped in another nowhere saloon in another nowhere town.

What did she expect? To look at her anyone with a lick of brains could see what she was. Ringlets of brown hair piled high on her head framed an attractive face, a face prematurely lined about the eyes and mouth, a face covered with enough kohl and coral to hide the shame and guilt she had long since learned to abide with. The blue-sateen bodice made sure her plump bosom was displayed for God and anyone to see until it damn near toppled right on out of her whale-boned corset. No one forced her to put her wares in front of men's drunken faces. No one forced her to brush her flesh against their cheeks and whisper satiny invitations into their ears. No one forced her to ply them with so much whiskey they couldn't tell the difference between getting their wick dipped and plain passin' out before their Peacemaker fired its rounds.

No one forced her to do anything.

No one but herself.

She fought back an urge to weep and, drawing a jerky breath, steeled her emotions, chin lifting. One thing wasn't her fault: the sparse business in the saloon tonight. She'd tried her best to entice some of those men, but they were more interested in poker than company.

Her gaze skipped about the barroom, landing anywhere but on the barman. Durham smoke hung heavy in the air and the reek of old vomit, cheap booze and liberally applied perfume made her nostrils twitch. The other girls, all two of them, were having no better luck, even Chinadoll. She reckoned Bessie was plug ugly, the poor thing, and usually got the leftovers and most beatings because of it. She had a face like a mule, stringy mouse-colored hair and was missing most of her lower teeth. Chinadoll, the Asian gal, was a different story. The exotic dove had pale porcelain skin that was almost white after she applied a coat of make-up, a small shapely figure, dark almond eyes and blue-black hair that a fella could almost see his reflection in. Men went for her the most, but even she was coming up short. She wouldn't be in as much danger from Perkins's fists and Coralie didn't know if that was because of her doll-like looks or because Chinadoll wielded a snapdragon temper.

Perkins, twisting at his handle-bar mustache, cast her a venomous look that told her she damn well better start making some money. A sinking feeling in her belly, she looked at two men hunched over their poker hands at a nearby table.

Forcing down an urge to vomit, she went over to the first man, leaning in so he could get a good eyeful of her womanly charms. He grinned but showed no other interest in what she had to offer; she wasn't sure whether to be more afraid or relieved.

As she straightened, an unguarded longing filled her mind with will-o'-the-wisp thoughts. Just once she wished she could go back and make things different, have a future that included a home and family with a decent man who cared about her. A man who loved and worshipped her, the way a woman wanted to be worshipped, for herself and not for how many delights could be paid for.

Hell, what was she thinkin'? She was a whore and that's all she'd ever be. She'd just damned well better accept it.

'Do not worry, Coralie.' The voice came from beside her and she all but jumped out of her corset. She hadn't heard the woman come up. 'You will find someone before the night is through.' It was meant to be comforting yet provided no solace. She patted the small white hand resting on her shoulder and turned to give Chinadoll a hug for caring in her own way. They had become sisters of a sort, and the Asian woman was the only whore she'd ever gotten close to.

'Reckon you're right, but sometimes I just don't want this any more . . .'

The black-haired woman frowned. 'Better you do not speak that way. You know how Perkins will respond to such talk. Besides, what else is there for us, Coralie? We are what we are.'

'Ain't there more? Ain't there somethin' better'n letting men touch us night after night?'

The Asian woman tried to smile but the expression was wooden. 'Does it matter? It is too late to decide not to be a whore.'

'Reckon there's a part of me that says it's never too late.'

The Chinese girl laughed a sarcastic laugh. 'That is a foolish thought, Coralie. No decent man would have us.'

'That don't mean it's too late to be free of this life.'

'My life ended when my master forced me to do what I do now, only he kept all the money while I kept my humiliation. That will not happen again. He beat me one too many times and I killed him when he fell asleep drunk. I am free now. The choice is mine and I keep what I earn.'

Coralie stared at the girl in befuddlement. For the life of her she couldn't see how Chinadoll could view saloon life as freedom.

'How you figure that?' She ducked her chin at the barkeep, who was staring at them, getting ready to come over and tell them to work their asses, most likely. 'He takes half of what we make an' beats the hell out of us when we don't bring in enough.'

Chinadoll laughed again. 'I keep half, now. Before I kept nothing. He will not beat me because he knows I will feed his balls to him if he tries.'

'That what makes it freedom?'

A confused light played in the Asian woman's dark eyes. 'I do not understand you so much, Coralie. It is not whoring that is wrong, it is not getting a share of the profit.'

An aching sadness welled in her heart. Many a time, in

dreams, she had thought of running away from all this, trying to start over somewhere else, but she had never mustered the courage to actually see it through. At least she had those dreams, however unlikely and broken. At least she knew the difference. Chinadoll did not.

Coralie barely recollected her pa, but somehow he had instilled something inside her that gave her dreams, something passionate and desiring that had survived the hell she'd endured the past fifteen years. Chinadoll had nothing but a slave existence with which to compare this life; maybe against that background black looked white.

A sound intruded on her reverie. It came from beyond the batwings, rising above the low murmur and staccato laughter. She glanced in that direction, the night outside appearing pitch black against the dim lantern-light of the saloon.

Horses, a number of them, and in Danton that was unusual. Shouts halting the mounts punctuated the air and for no reason she could pinpoint dread blossomed in the back of her mind. Chinadoll's attention focused on the batwings as well and Perkins's face gilded with greed at the prospect of more customers.

The clinking of spurs reached her ears, followed by heavy bootfalls. Closer. The dread in her mind strengthened and for the life her she couldn't tell why.

A moment later she understood. A moment later the batwings parted and the Devil stood in the doorway.

She had never seen such a man. Large of frame and wide of shoulder, he seemed to exude a presence of evil that made her shiver and raised gooseflesh across her bosom. A patch covered one eye and a hook protruded from his coat-sleeve where his left hand should have been. Another shudder came as his gaze fell upon her, lusting and cruel, and she clung to Chinadoll's arm.

'That man . . .' Chinadoll's voice came out a whisper.

'You know him?' Coralie couldn't take her gaze from the figure.

'I have heard ... *things*. He is a bad one. He takes women and kills without remorse. The papers, they call him the Buccaneer.'

'He's a mean-lookin' sonofabitch, that's for sure.'

The man stepped deeper into the saloon, five others filtering in behind him. 'Well, hell, mateys, don't stop the revelry on my account!' His shout made her jolt and she held tighter to Chinadoll.

The one-eyed man gazed about the room, and men froze, cards in hand. Perkins's face exchanged greed for fear. 'Where the hell is Crawford? He was s'posed to meet us at this here saloon after he got done making sure that old man didn't put no one on our trail.'

A man to the leader's right shrugged. 'Maybe he's upstairs gettin' pants rats.' The man snickered.

'Shut the hell up, Higgins.' With a sudden explosive move he swung his hook, catching the edge of a table and throwing it over. It landed with a crash and the snickering gang-member's mouth clamped shut. Bessie, standing next to the table, let out a surprised bleat.

'Didn't mean nothin' by it, Morgan.' A terrified look crossed Higgins's face and he cast a glance at the leader's hook.

'Any more women upstairs?' Morgan's gaze drilled Perkins, who shook his head.

Perkins made a mistake after the outlaw's eye turned away from him, a fatal one. Coralie saw it, and despite her hatred of the man tried to yell at him to stop, but couldn't make her voice work.

Perkins reached beneath the counter where Coralie knew he kept a scatter-gun. He didn't make it halfway before the outlaw leader, watching from the corner of his eye, shifted sideways and drew the sword at his waist. The blade flashed up and Perkins froze in a half-crouch, uttering a stifled gasp as the tip of the cutlass pressed into his Adam's apple.

'Now, you don't really want to do that, do you?' The man with the patch nudged the tip forward and blood trickled down the 'keep's throat. A vindictive notion made Coralie wonder if Perkins enjoyed feeling fear as much as he liked doling it out.

'I asked you a question, whelp.' The leader twisted the blade, drawing more blood, and Perkins tried to shake his head.

'Nooo.' The plea came from Bessie, whose trembling hands went to her mouth.

The bandit let out a corrosive laugh and shoved the blade through Perkins's throat.

The bartender, choking, blood bubbling from his lips and spouting from the wound, staggered backward as the outlaw yanked the blade free. He slammed into a hutch filled with bottles and collapsed behind the bar. Glass shattered about him. Bile shot into Coralie's throat and she had all she could do not to vomit. Chinadoll's arms went around her waist, steadying her, but even the exotic dove's face bleached bone-white.

Bessie lost any remaining composure and began shrieking.

The man with the patch gazed at her, brow knitting, then replaced the cutlass in its sheath after wiping the blood off on his pant leg. He drew his Smith & Wesson and aimed it at the dove, whose shrieks filled with mortal terror.

'You're plug ugly. I don't need you.' He pulled the trigger and crimson exploded across Bessie's peek-a-boo blouse. She flew backward like a rag doll flung aside by a careless child and crashed to the floor, unmoving.

Tears burned in Coralie's eyes. 'Oh no, oh no . . .' Her

voice came low, choked with emotion. Perkins's death had sickened her, but Bessie's made her heart wither.

The other bandits drew guns and leveled them at the men sitting around the tables in case any took a notion to resist.

The man with the patch swung his gun to the back of the bar, blasting away at the few bottles remaining in the hutch. Glass exploded and rained to the floor. Liquor sprayed the walls. Acrid blue smoke hung in the air and the roar of gunfire thundered in Coralie's ears.

The events took only heartbeats but to her it seemed an eternity. Fear, nausea, grief overwhelmed her. She struggled to keep her senses as the room spun and blackness threatened to sweep her into unconsciousness. She was vaguely aware of Chinadoll shaking her, trying to keep her from passing out.

Silence, sudden, deafening.

Holstering his gun, the outlaw leader came forward, gaze pinning her and Chinadoll. Viciousness glittered in that dark eye, something not even human, and with that gaze came the frightening realization that evil was not some devil preached about in Sunday sermons; it was a man, this man, and even God in Heaven would not stop him from his intended task here tonight.

He grabbed the Asian woman's arm and looked back to his men. Chinadoll winced, let out a mew of pain, as his fingers gouged into her flesh. 'This here whore's right different, ain't she, boys?' He looked back to her. 'She's one of them chinks I heard about. Reckon she'll fetch a right nice price.'

'You go to hell, you bastard!' Chinadoll spat at the man and Coralie's belly plunged. She wanted to slap the girl, tell her to keep her mouth shut this once so he didn't kill her.

The outlaw jerked her closer, tearing her from Coralie's

arms. 'Course, we're gonna have to break her first.' He whirled her around and sent her sailing towards one of his men, who caught her. She struggled, but he held her fast and dragged her from the barroom. The remaining bandits, as if on some unspoken command, went to tables and began scooping up silver dollars and greenbacks.

Coralie tried to go after Chinadoll but the leader grabbed her, flinging her at a table. She crashed against it, the edge jamming into the small of her back and sending welts of pain down her legs. She tried to grab for the derringer tucked deep in her skirt pocket, but he was on her too fast. He backhanded her, a stunning blow that rocked her head and spilt her lip. Variegated stars exploded before her eyes and she felt herself falling backward, atop the table. Her mind reeled and for a moment she couldn't tell what was happening.

Then it suddenly became all too clear.

Cold lips pressed against her own in a violent kiss. Gagging, she fought to get out from beneath him, but he was too powerful.

He hoisted her skirt and tore at her bodice. She bit at his lips and tried to jam her knee where it would do the most damage. He ended that by smashing a fist against her temple. She went limp, unable to raise her hands or fight him off. Only by some sinful whim of Hell did she remain aware of him taking her.

When it was over, he left her sprawled across the table. She grew aware of muffled sounds around her, blurred motion, men yelling and moving about, bootfalls, spurs clinking, and at one point shots. She struggled to sit up, but rolled off the table, hitting the floor hard enough to mercifully bring unconsciousness.

When she regained her senses, a man was helping her into a chair. Another man was lying on the floor in a pool of blood.

'Wanted to hold on to his bloody pocket-watch,' the cowboy helping her said, as her horrified gaze settled on the body. 'Said his wife gave it to him and he wouldn't part with it. They took it anyway, the sonsofbitches.'

She nodded, half understanding. Around her the few men left alive headed for the batwings, likely to fetch the marshal. She saw no sign of the outlaws or Chinadoll. They had taken her with them and if it were possible for a woman such as her to lose any more of her self-respect, they had taken that with them, too.

THREE

The first blood-and-amber rays of sunlight arced through the boarding-house window and sliced across the dusty floorboards. In another few moments the light would creep across Trace McCoy's boots, which he had not bothered to remove last night after collapsing into the overstuffed chair angled into a corner of his room. Not having moved from the chair since sundown, he'd stared into the shimmering darkness, obsessing over the events in the barroom and castigating himself for burying his only lead.

Now he had nothing.

Five years was an eternity to search for justice and he refused to wait another five to discover the fate of John Harrigan and avenge Karen's death. He would put a bullet through his brains long before that happened.

Christamighty, he missed her.

Some things just shouldn't last forever and missing a loved one was one of them.

Where could he go from here? Was that hardcase his only hope? Was John Harrigan indeed alive?

He prayed the sonofabitch still lived; if this God-forsaken world held even a lick of justice that man would die by Trace McCoy's hand.

Shifting in the chair, muscles tight from remaining in one position for so long, he sifted through the few known facts for the hundredth time. The dead man had been heading south for the past week and appeared to be searching for something, but did a man like that move with rhyme or reason? Was he even still a member of the Harrigan gang or had he struck out on his own after the outlaw met with some unknown doom? Those answers lay beneath a sheet at the funeral man's office.

Half an hour after returning to his room, Trace had heard a knock on his door. The marshal questioned him without much conviction, already in possession of a statement from the saloon man tagging the killing as self-defense. No charges would be pressed.

The sun's rays softened to gold, highlighting the dark hollows about his eyes and the grief-chiseled lines of his face. While not an old man, barely a shade past thirty-three, experience and suffering had set more years to his hide than a body deserved. In five years he had aged twenty.

Help me . . .

A gasp slipped from his lips. His fingers dug into the arms of the chair as her plea rose from the depths of his mind. A wave of anguish washing over him, the nightmare of that day struggled to overwhelm his senses. He fought the images away for not the first time since the marshal departed yesterday afternoon.

Damn Rutherford Chadburn for only making matters worse.

Dwelling on the railroad man's desperate request, Trace cursed the mocking voice of his conscience that scolded him for turning down the job. He knew how Chadburn felt, losing his daughter, knew it only too well. The disbelief, the anger, the loss.

What if you can save her?

Was there a possibility of finding Violet Chadburn alive? Of bringing her kidnapper to justice and easing the railroad man's pain in a way Trace's own could never be? That separated the two of them, didn't it? Chadburn had a chance at getting back what he'd lost; Trace did not. That realization flooded him with an irrational resentment for the old man.

He had no right to feel that way, though he reckoned it was just another moment of weakness in a life riddled with many. The old man deserved his compassion and empathy, not his bitterness. It was too goddamned easy to let hate spill over sometimes, be directed at others, but if it served any purpose at all it brought him to a conclusion regarding the man's plight. Yesterday, in turning down Chadburn's appeal, he had reacted out of anger and discouragement, letting the darkness in his soul cloud his compassion. He had been wrong and he knew it. He had a chance to make things right for one man, though he could never make them right for himself. That's what had driven him to become a manhunter in the first place, one of the soulless killers who tracked hardcases. It was the only thing a man named Trace McCoy had done right in five years.

He leaned forward, putting his face in hands, haunted by emotion and the past. Karen would want him to find Violet Chadburn. The girl was out there, somewhere, alone, and, if alive, likely frightened and hanging on the slim hope her father would send someone to find her. Someone like Trace McCoy.

He pushed away the thoughts and stood, going to the bed and grabbing his rig from where he had left it slung over a post. After strapping it around his waist, he slid the gun in and out of the holster; the weapon felt comforting in his grip, an old friend.

What if that man's daughter's dead?

That was one question he did have an answer for: he would kill the murderer and deliver his body to Rutherford Chadburn. At least the railroad man would have an end to his search, if not his suffering.

What if you don't find her? What if her killer escapes the way Harrigan did?

The notion made something in his belly cinch but he refused to think about that, at least for the time being. His trail was five years old; Chadburn's was fresh and that made the odds far better.

What do you do after that, McCoy?

He drew his Peacemaker, peering long and hard at the barrel and wondering whether he'd finally have the courage to place it to his temple and pull the trigger, or whether he'd simply delude himself one more time into believing there was still a chance Harrigan was alive and justice would be served.

He slid the six-shooter back into its holster, swallowing at a bitter taste in his mouth.

'Coward . . .' he whispered, then headed for the door.

The saloon was empty at this time of morning, except for the 'keep, a bar dove who served breakfast and one other man sitting at a table with his back to Trace. He paused, gaze taking in the interior and going to the spot where the hardcase's body had lain, as quickly looking away. He didn't need to dwell on defeat, not if he were going to find Chadburn's daughter.

Stepping up to the bar, Trace tossed a silver dollar on to the counter. 'Whiskey.'

The 'keep cocked an eyebrow. 'Bit early to start drinkin', ain't it?'

'You the temperance committee, now?' Trace's tone came bitter and the barman shrugged, setting a glass on the counter, then grabbing a bottle from the hutch and pouring the drink.

'Gals serve breakfast since the café burned down.

Reckon that'd be better than rotgut first thing in the morning. Hell, you ain't the only one lookin' to drown your sorrows, though.' The 'keep ducked his chin at the lone customer. Trace nodded, scooping up his glass and moving away from the counter.

As he reached the table, the other man glanced up at him with a haggard expression.

'Looks like I ain't the only one who spent the night awake, Chadburn.'

The railroad man laughed, a brittle, lifeless sound. 'What reason would you have to lose sleep, Mr McCoy? Your conscience is clear, is it not?'

Trace frowned, dragging out a chair and lowering himself on to it. 'Reckon I deserve that, but I got more reason than you think.' The older man peered at him, as if searching for something in Trace's eyes. Rutherford Chadburn was a man used to reading others, ordering them about, but likely fair in his judgments. From what Trace had heard of him, he elicited loyalty among his workers and had a heavy approval rating where threading rail was concerned. Rumor had it the man might run for office. But not the defeated half-drunk man before Trace now. Not the man without a daughter.

'Maybe you do, Mr McCoy . . .' His voice quivered, and he took another drink of his whiskey. 'Maybe you do . . .'

Trace downed a swig of his own drink then reached into his pocket, pulling out the velvet pouch of dominoes and untying the drawstrings. He dumped the bones on to the table and began turning them face down. 'Tell me about your daughter, Mr Chadburn.'

A spark of hope ignited in the older man's eyes, but Trace kept his gaze on the pieces. 'You saw her likeness, Mr McCoy. She was . . . *is* exquisite, the prettiest and sweetest girl this side of heaven. She's everything to me, all a father could want. She was to be married next year.'

'Why'd she came West? Don't hardly seem the place for a delicate woman.'

A thin smile appeared on the railroad man's lips.

'Unfortunately she inherited my stubborn streak. I told her not to come, tried to convince her that the West was no place for a city woman, but she paid me no mind. I got a telegram informing she was on her way and there was nothing I could do to stop it. I reckon it's my own fault. After her mother passed on, I tried to shield her, remove every obstacle from her path. Maybe I shouldn't have doted over her so much because it just made her more determined to experience the things I tried to protect her from.'

Trace flipped over a line of seven dominoes, then began selecting pieces from the boneyard and placed them in descending numbers beneath the queue. 'She was traveling West to spite you?'

Chadburn uttered a feeble laugh. 'Maybe that had something to do with it, but I think she truly wanted to see what she was missing. I told her Colorado was full of hardship and danger. I grew up near the Pecos, Mr McCoy. I knew the West was unforgiving, no place for any man or woman unprepared for the reality of lawless towns and ruthless bandits, Indians.'

'Yet you came back . . .'

'I had no choice. I own a railroad company, a company laying track across this nation.'

'Whoever attacked her coach left the drivers and a gambler dead?' Trace focused on the domino numbers but listened intently to the railroad man's every word.

'Took all their possessions, too, pocket-watches, cash. Marshal found one driver down the trail, the other slumped in the seat. Both had been shot.'

'And the gambler?'

'He was lying on the ground. Marshal said looked like he had been run through with a sword or the like.'

Trace's gaze lifted. 'Sword?'

The older man nodded. 'You read the papers much lately?'

'Not if I can help it. Ain't much news I care to hear any more.' Trace recollected reading them all at one time, years ago; in fact he had scoured them for any clue that would point to Harrigan, but had given up after the outlaw disappeared.

'Few towns 'round these parts been hit by a gang the papers call the Buccaneers.'

'Pirates?' Trace flipped over another piece, frowning.

'From witnesses' accounts, the few left alive, the leader wears an eyepatch and has a hook instead of a hand. Carries a sword, too. Reckon it was his gang who took my daughter.'

Trace nodded, not quite knowing how much stock to put in that. Papers were known to exaggerate or plain make up things and with outlaw gangs rumors were wont to fly. 'Say this gang did take your daughter, why? They killed three other men yet not her?'

The railroad man's face darkened. 'I don't know the answer to that, Mr McCoy, but it ain't the first time a woman's been taken by this gang. From what I could learn they kidnap mostly whores. Hear they take the prettiest. A few decent women have disappeared from their homes, too.'

'You do your research, Mr Chadburn.' Trace dropped the domino in his hand when he saw he had no further moves. Losing again, he let out a disgusted *pfft*, scooped up the pieces and slid them into the pouch.

Chadburn's voice lowered. 'I only wish I had discovered more.'

'Ain't a lot to go on, is it?' Trace tucked the pouch into his pocket.

'No, I am afraid it isn't, but I *will* find them, Mr McCoy. I swear I will.'

'You won't have to, Mr Chadburn.'

The man's gaze locked with Trace's, the spark of hope glittering brighter. 'Are you saying you'll help me?'

Trace nodded. 'Reckon I was plannin' on coming to your hotel room after I got done here, but you saved me the trouble.'

The man took a roll of greenbacks from his coat pocket and placed them on the table in front of Trace. The manhunter peered at them and shook his head.

'I don't understand. I thought you intended to take the case.' Confusion and disappointment spread across Chadburn's face.

'I do. You provided your daughter the best of everything, Chadburn, but some gals don't get that chance. Help one of them if I find your daughter.'

The railroad man nodded, understanding. 'Just find her, Mr McCoy. Please.'

'I ain't makin' no promises but I'll do my best to bring her back to you.'

Trace stood, running his finger along the scar on his chin. 'These men, these pirates, they got any pattern you can see?'

The railroad man shrugged. 'Near as I can tell they strike around a fifty-mile radius in these parts.'

'Where was your daughter s'posed to meet you?'

'Danton. I got an office there.'

'That's about a half-day's ride.'

Chadburn nodded. 'I came north to find you. My sources told me you had been seen in Lockwood. You aren't exactly unknown in Colorado, Mr McCoy. A man in your profession ain't hard to locate.'

Trace let out a grunt. ''Lot's been written about me in those dime novels and papers, Mr Chadburn; I don't read 'em but likely most of what they say ain't true.'

Chadburn looked at him, intensity in his eyes. 'They say

you are ruthless and something happened long ago that killed your compassion.'

Trace sighed. 'Well, maybe they got me pegged better than I thought.'

The railroad man shook his head. 'No, Mr McCoy. Yesterday I might have called you a heartless bastard. But I was wrong. You got compassion or you wouldn't be helping me. I can see that now. And I see something else in your eyes. I don't know what demon's got a hold of you, but I hope you find a way to best it.'

Trace's gaze held the older man's for a suspended moment, then he turned away, at a loss for words. Rutherford Chadburn read men too damn well.

A brassy sun blazed high overhead by the time Trace McCoy rode into Danton. Sweat trickled from his brow and he couldn't deny the weariness in his bones from a night without sleep. The day was warm for mid-October and the air carried an odor of decaying leaves. He hated that scent; it reminded him of death. He prayed it was not an omen that pointed toward the fate of Violet Chadburn.

Although he hadn't told the old man, he had caught rumors of the Buccaneer gang, and of the outlaw who led them. Whispered things mostly, in saloons, uttered by cowboys deep in their cups. He'd paid them little mind, though admittedly the talk had piqued his manhunter's curiosity. A time or two he half considered looking into the rumors to keep himself from going loco with self-pity, but spotting the Harrigan gang member had erased any thoughts of West-born pirates.

Sifting through all the railroad man told him, he found himself nagged by the lack of solid leads to the young woman's kidnappers. Was the railroad man simply relying on rumor and linking it to his daughter's vanishing in a desperate hope for a clue to her whereabouts? After all, the man was basing his evidence solely on the fact that a gambler had been killed by a sword. Still, Trace was inclined to believe there was something to the fellow's conclusions. Was a pirate band the concoction of reporters eager to feed a West hungry for myth? Call it manhunter's intuition, or the fact that Chadburn, no matter how distraught over his daughter's vanishing, wasn't the type to chase will-o'-the-wisps, but Trace accepted the fact the gang existed and had taken a hand in the abduction.

While armed with few tangible facts in the case, one thing was certain: women were missing. What would such a gang want with them? If they simply were inclined to keep whores or take what they needed from helpless women forcefully, surely bodies would have turned up by now. Granted, the West was a huge place and a corpse could disappear forever if a murderer saw fit, but outlaws weren't known for their tidiness. Since the gang flaunted their activity, it wasn't likely they would take the time to bury their victims or give a damn about them being discovered.

Which meant they had some other purpose for them, one he couldn't name. Yet.

After talking to Chadburn again before leaving, Trace decided the best place to start was Danton, Violet's destination. He had no other prospects at the moment and hoped if he questioned the marshal there he would discover something the railroad man didn't know, though that was a long shot.

Danton, a small town of clapboard buildings and a latticelike affair of streets, stood to mushroom once the rail came through. On the wide main street lined with false-front buildings, he noted a saloon, general store and various businesses. The railroad man's office was down-street to the left. The earthy scents of dust and manure, baked under the Colorado sun, assailed his nostrils. The atmosphere seemed somehow darker than it should have, somber, and he wondered if that meant anything. A look of tense seriousness gripped the faces of the few out and about, put stiffness in their strides.

He held his horse to a slow walk, his gaze roving. Locating the marshal's office, he guided his bay to the rail and dismounted, looping the reins around the beam. He cast a final look over the street, the strange sense of disquiet strengthening. Something was wrong, but he couldn't pinpoint what. Perhaps the fact that more people should be about in at town like this or . . .

Fear? Yes, that was it. Subtle but there, some undefined anxiety. Had something happened in this town? Did it somehow relate to his search for Violet Chadburn?

An older man sitting behind a worn desk looked up with a startled look as Trace entered the office and the sense of darkness he'd felt in the street became solid. Fear played in the marshal's eyes, but why?

'Marshal . . .' Trace nodded to the man as he closed the door behind him.

The marshal's hand drifted below the desk and Trace knew the man was resting his fingers on the butt of his gun. From the looks of him the lawdog was little used to doing much more than chasing down pie-stealers. Round as any man could be, he was bald except for tufts of steel-gray hair sticking out of either side of his head. His chins numbered three more than the one God had provided him.

'Who are you, stranger?' His voice came challenging and Trace noticed a line of sweat beading across the man's creased forehead.

'Don't lose your water, Marshal. Name's Trace McCoy.'

The man arched an eyebrow. 'The manhunter?'

'You heard of me?'

'Who ain't?'

'Wish I could say everyone.'

The marshal underwent a visible transformation. Tenseness drained from his face and his hand came back up to the desk top. He heaved his bulk from the chair, coming around the desk and reaching for Trace's hand. Trace accepted the gesture and the lawdog, palm slick with moisture, pumped his hand furiously.

'Mighty glad to see you in these parts, sir, mighty glad.'

'I get the impression you were expecting someone else, maybe someone you didn't want to meet up with.'

The man nodded, chins bouncing, then went back to his desk and collapsed into his chair, as if the very act of greeting Trace had exhausted him.

'I ain't ashamed to tell ya I'm mighty glad it's you and not them other fellas again.' His beadlike eyes, sunk deep in pouches of gristle, glittered with fear. This man had no call being a lawdog in Trace's estimation. He was lucky he hadn't gotten his ticket punched way before now.

'What fellas?'

'Why, them pirates. They hit the Silver Horseshoe saloon last night. Killed the 'keep and another man and one of the girls. Took another.'

While Trace had been hoping for a lead to the gang, this was more than he could have expected. 'You sure about them bein' the pirate gang? You see them?'

'Hell, no!' The man's words came so violently sweat flew in a spray from his forehead. 'But Coralie, she saw them. So did a couple fellas they left alive.'

'Where can I find this Coralie?'

The lawdog shrugged, the move appearing to take an enormous amount of effort. 'Reckon I wouldn't know now that the saloon's empty. She used to have a room upstairs but you know whores. They're like to move on the minute trouble starts.'

Trace uttered a small laugh, thinking maybe the marshal would do well to consider doing the same. That gang came back he suspected the lawdog couldn't have gotten out of his chair fast enough to save anyone, let alone his own hide.

Going to the door and placing a hand on the handle, he gazed at the lawman. 'You don't mind a piece of advice, maybe you should consider retiring. Marshalin' can be a right dangerous profession.'

The man's round face blanched. 'Been chewin' on that very thought, Mr McCoy. This used to be a right peaceful town.' The man's brow crinkled. 'Say, McCoy. . . ?'

'Yeah, Marshal?'

'You're goin' after them pirates, aint ya? I mean, a fella like you's just what the doc ordered.'

McCoy gave a small laugh and left without answering.

Standing on the edge of the boardwalk, he gazed out at the street, attention centering on the Silver Horseshoe saloon. He wondered whether the dove named Coralie had left town or, if here, whether she could tell him any more than he already learned. Coming to Danton had provided him with confirmation the gang existed and that they were indeed taking women. That made the case for Violet Chadburn all the more probable. Beyond that, however, was he in a much better position than when he had ridden in?

He sighed and crossed the street to the saloon. Pushing through the batwings, he stood just inside. With the owner dead, no one had bothered to close up the place.

The interior was gloomy. Sunlight arced through dusty windows, providing a ghostly atmosphere that wasn't lost to him. The feeling that death had visited, leaving behind only emptiness and despair, permeated the barroom.

Sawdust ground beneath his boots as he stepped deeper into the saloon. He noted overturned tables and

chairs, along with browning splotches of dried blood stain-
ing the floorboards. A hint of copper soured the air,
mixed with old booze and stale smoke. Flies buzzed
around the bloodstains.

He stopped suddenly as a sob reached his ears.

At the back of the barroom a staircase rose to an upper
level. A woman dressed in a satin bodice and skirt sat
hunched on one of the steps about halfway up, her face
buried in her hands. She likely hadn't even noticed his
entrance.

He walked to the bottom of the stairs and removed his
hat, having no wish to startle her, but knowing this woman
was likely the dove, Coralie, and he needed to question
her about what had happened.

'Ma'am?' He tried to keep his voice as soothing as he
could, but hadn't had a hell of a lot of practice talking to
women in the past five years, so it came out more abrupt
than he intended.

Her head jerked up, fear lashing her face. Streaks of
kohl ran from her widened eyes and her coral-daubed
cheeks were smudged. Dark pouches nested beneath her
bloodshot eyes. But behind the fear, beneath the pancake,
she reminded him vaguely of Karen, the hair color, the
high cheekbones and turn of lip. It gave him pause, resur-
rected ghosts that made him uncomfortable.

'What do you want?' Her voice trembled, but came with
a harsh challenge.

'You Coralie?'

She studied him, nodded. 'Who are you?'

'Name's Trace McCoy, I'm—'

'I heard of you. Your name goes around saloons.'

He nodded. 'What happened here, ma'am?'

She sniffled, shuddering as a storm of pain washed
across her eyes. 'Men came in last night . . . awful men.'

'Dressed like pirates?' He placed a foot on the first step,

bracing his hand on his thigh.

She shook her head. 'Only one of 'em. Wasn't so much dressed like one, just that he had himself an eyepatch and hook instead of a hand. Had a sword, too. Killed the barkeep with it.'

Trace considered her words. Her story all but confirmed what the railroad man said about the gambler's death.

'You saw this man personally?'

Anger flashed in her eyes. 'That's a right stupid question. Hell, yes, I saw him! Fact, I got a right close-up view. That man, he . . .' She hesitated, as if searching for words. 'He violated me and took a friend of mine with him.'

He studied her, knowing now why she had faltered. A woman who sold herself for money, she likely thought the notion of anyone violating her would bring a laugh from most folks. Trace found it anything but funny.

'They take her alive?'

She gave a jerky nod. 'One of the gang dragged her out. I don't know much of what happened after that man . . . took me.'

'You got a notion what they'd want with her?' He paused. 'And why they'd leave you?'

She shrugged, a sob wracking her frame. Tears rushed down her face and dripped on to her bosom, running dark gray with kohl. He noticed her clothing was torn in places. 'She was pretty, different, one of them Chinese girls. He killed Bessie because she wasn't so good lookin'. Guess he found me just passable enough to use and leave behind. I ain't ugly but I ain't a young pretty gal, either.'

He reckoned she wasn't that old, maybe twenty-five or six, but showed lines of wear around the eyes and mouth that aged her a bit beyond her years.

'You got any notion where they were headed?'

She shook her head. 'You hunt them types down, McCoy, don't you?'

He looked at the stair, then back to her, setting his hat on his head. 'Reckon you could say that.'

'Then I want to hire you. I want those men dead and I want my friend back.'

The notion of a bargirl hiring him struck him as unusual but he saw something in her eyes he seldom witnessed in others of her type: a compassion and raw integrity. A flashing curiosity made him wonder what had made her the way she was, but he quickly forced the thought away. Her life was none of his concern and that she resembled someone he loved in a passing way made no nevermind.

He turned and started towards the batwings. Likely he had learned all he could here. It confirmed his mission, nothing else.

The girl stood, with bleached fingers gripping the banister as though she would fall if she didn't hold on to something.

'I said I want to hire you, McCoy. Didn't you hear me?'

He stopped, not turning. 'I heard you, ma'am. I don't want your money.'

She started down the steps, leaning heavily against the rail as she descended. 'You think because I do what I do I should just accept the fact that man raped me, don't you? You think just because he kidnapped a whore it ain't important.' Anger laced her voice and he turned to see her narrowed eyes drilling him, accusing, pain-filled and somehow desperate. 'You won't help me because I am what I am.'

'That ain't it, ma'am.'

'Then what is it? I ain't no virtuous woman, Mr McCoy, but you ain't exactly a saint neither, are you?'

' 'Fraid I don't follow.' But he did and something about

it irked him. He wasn't used to barwomen making judgments on his profession.

'You follow. You damn well follow. You kill folks, McCoy. Maybe not in cold blood exactly, but how many fellas could you have taken alive if you wanted? What makes you want to kill them anyway? Most ain't none of your business like the men I see ain't none of mine. We both take our pay and live with what we did, don't we?'

He frowned, her words getting under his skin and making him feel a tinge of guilt for no reason he could figure. 'You're right about one thing, ma'am: some things ain't my business, like what you do.'

Her features grew indignant and she wrapped her arms about herself. 'Does what I do make me so much less than you, Mr McCoy? I ain't makin' no excuses for my life, but there's damn sure a difference between takin' pay for somethin' and havin' it forced on you. And no matter what Chinadoll was she don't deserve what those men might do to her.'

His gaze locked with hers and he nodded. 'You're right on that account, too.' Turning from her again, he went to the batwings and stepped out into the daylight. Behind him he heard the sound of her breaking down into sobs and hesitated, compassion struggling to take over and send him back inside to comfort her, tell her he was already looking for the men and if he found her friend, dead or alive, he would see to it he brought her back. But what call did he have consoling a woman like that – a woman who sold herself and took her chances where rough men were concerned? Did he feel sympathy solely because she reminded him of Karen? Or was it simply because whatever she was she was still a human being who felt and bled and grieved over the loss of a friend and it meant something human still lived somewhere deep inside of him?

Christamighty, this ain't the time to go soft, McCoy. That ain't part of the plan.

Only death and vengeance lived in his world, and possibly every so often a deed done that alleviated someone else's sorrow, but never his own.

He walked out into the street, the sounds of her sobs haunting him, but not enough to turn back.

FOUR

Dusk sketched the land with gray shadows and opal moonshine. The sounds of katydids rose in a gleeful chorus with the glassy bubbling of the stream that paralleled the trail. After tethering his horse to a cottonwood branch, Trace gathered an armful of brush and branches, then coaxed a fire to life. He held his palms towards the blaze, fingers numb from the chill that came with the sunset.

An hour later, he'd laid out his bedroll and swallowed a meal of hardtack and jerky, washing it down with coffee strong enough to be redeye.

He lowered himself cross-legged to the ground before the flames, a measure of disappointment gripping him. He had wasted much of the afternoon searching the trail where the stage had been held up, coming up empty.

Convinced nothing remained to be found in Danton, he'd headed south before a nagging guilt sent him back to the saloon to console the bargirl, Coralie. Hell, what did he care about a woman he'd never laid eyes on before today? A whore to boot! Christamighty, guilt had turned into a constant companion the past couple days. What the Sam Hill was the matter with him?

Maybe you're finally comin' apart at the seams you sonofabitch . . .

59

Was that it? Had the years of single-minded determination to find and kill Harrigan caught up with him and made him loco? Or had another failure snuffed the spark of hope that kept him going?

As he stared into the jittering flames, emotion tightened his throat and he shook his head, forcing the image of that dead hardcase from his mind. He needed to focus on the job at hand, somehow convince himself he would discover another lead and continue along the vengeance trail after he located Chadburn's daughter.

Lazarette lay another half-day's ride south. If the pirates were holed up in that direction, it made sense they would hit the town first. With any luck, he would interrupt their plans, though they had a hell of a head start. He should have ridden through the night but his horse was damn near as exhausted as its rider.

Drawing his knees to his chest, he pressed his brow against his forearms, a wave of depression washing over him. He had little chance of shaking it until justice was done, but was retribution even enough to assuage the bitter empty man he had become?

A dark thought made him consider placing the gun at his hip to his temple. How easy it would be to just step off this world and be with her.

You can't do it, McCoy. You don't have the guts . . .

A sound invaded his reverie and his head jerked up. He came to his feet, ears pricked.

The sound came a second time, a horse snorting, not his own, then hoof-falls, drawing closer. No doubt attracted by the fire, someone was approaching his camp and making little attempt at stealth.

While he doubted the rider posed much threat, he got a cottonwood between him and the direction of the trail just in case. He slid the Peacemaker from its holster and held it raised, close to his cheek.

Holding his breath, he waited, itching to pull the trigger. Sometimes that desire came all too easy. He killed men he could have taken alive, but hell they were all guilty. Why leave anything to chance? He wouldn't have them escape or somehow wrangle their way out of justice because of some silver-tongued lawyer. That rightly didn't make the fact he enjoyed seeing those men pay for their crimes any less truthful. Every one of those men had worn the face of John Harrigan and every one of them died as though responsible for Karen's death.

Christ, what was wrong with him? He had no call letting such thoughts distract his attention while someone was riding into his camp. He *was* going loco, plain and simple.

At the edge of the clearing a rider came into the light and Trace frowned. Holstering his gun, he stepped from behind the tree.

'What the hell're you doin' here?' His gaze settled on the girl in the saddle.

Still dressed in the torn bodice and skirt, she cast him a perturbed look. 'I ain't in the habit of havin' men greet me that way, Mr McCoy. They're usually right pleased to see me.'

'Then make this a first, 'cause I ain't pleased.'

Her questioning look made it obvious his reaction puzzled her. He was a man and he reckoned she thought she had them all pegged.

'You sure know how to make a gal feel welcome, don't you?' Her voice carried a sarcastic edge.

'Ain't my place to make you feel anything but the need to turn around and head right back where you came from.'

She smiled, but the expression came forced, practiced, automatic; it pegged her more as what she was than the kohl-smeared eyes and coral smudged on her cheeks. Ignoring him, she stepped from the saddle and stood beside the horse, gripping the reins.

'Where I came from ain't got nothin' for me now. Thought I made that clear.'

He sighed and ducked his chin at her bodice and skirt. 'Those your ridin' clothes?'

'I left the saloon in a hurry. Didn't have time to pack no clothes, food, neither. I saw you ride out. I got me a horse from the livery man with the last of the money I had and rode after you.'

'I must be slippin'.' Or too preoccupied with self-pity, he scolded himself.

What might have been a genuine smile turned her lips. 'Might say the only thing my ma ever taught me was how to be sneaky. I figured you'd head to Lazarette. It's the next town along this trail and I stayed far enough behind so you wouldn't see me. But you must have stopped some-where 'cause you damn near stumbled over me on the trail.'

'Was looking for somethin' north of here.'

She nodded, then led her horse to the tree and looped the reins around a branch.

'You find whatever it was?'

He peered at her as she came up to him. The firelight softened her features, fluttered in her eyes and glossed her too-red lips. 'What the hell you think you're doin'?' He nudged his head at the horse. She made an attempt at a coy laugh, but failed.

'Why, goin' along with you, Mr McCoy. Now don't worry 'bout it lookin' decent, I ain't been concerned about my honor in years.'

'Why the devil would you want to go with me?' His brow crinkled.

'Because I want you to find that man who violated me and took my friend, Mr McCoy.'

'Reckon you best get right back on that horse and go

back to Danton. This ain't no place for a . . .' The words caught and he wasn't sure why.

'A what, Mr McCoy? You don't have to worry 'bout my sensibilities.'

'A woman, I was gonna say.'

She moved closer and the scent of her perfume flooded his senses, making his belly flutter. 'You think I'm pretty, Mr McCoy?' Her tone had changed, become inviting, her look coy. Although he knew it was merely a costume she wore for men in bars, something about her struck him as damn appealing and things stirred inside of him he had no business feeling.

Her hands drifted to the top of her bodice and she slipped it down, revealing herself to him.

He swallowed hard, legs going weak. 'Ma'am, I . . .'

'You do find me desirable, Mr McCoy, don't you?'

Hell, yes! he almost blurted, but better judgment prevented him from taking total leave of his composure. He damn well had to admit it was a struggle.

'Put your bodice back on.' He took a backward step, using as much care as possible because his legs were rubbery and the slightest miscalculation would cause him to trip over his own feet.

The expression of coyness vanished and her face hardened. Any look of passion in her eyes dissolved, replaced by desperation, anger and maybe even a measure of hurt.

'Hell, this is all I got to offer a gent, McCoy. It's all I ever had. I got no money. You don't want me, I got no way to make you take me with you and find Chinadoll.'

'You sell yourself plumb short, then. What you got to offer don't come from outside. Maybe it's about time you realized that.'

'You don't want me?' The hurt bleeding into her eyes was likely the first honest emotion she had shown him. In that instant the woman before him was no longer a prac-

ticed whore, but a young woman desperate for some sort
of validation, someone who needed to be needed and
maybe he owed that some honesty of his own.

'Hell, yes, everything that makes me a man is tellin' me
I want you. But I don't want what's bought and paid for. I
been alone a long while but I ain't never consorted
with . . .'

'A whore, Mr McCoy? You might as well say it. Ain't like
I haven't been called worse.'

'Call it whatever you want, but I ain't about to pay no
disrespect to her memory that way.'

'Whose memory, Mr McCoy?'

The question stopped him dead and he suddenly realized he had revealed so much to a woman he barely knew,
a woman any man would likely be a fool to trust. She sold
herself for money, pandered to whatever would work to
her advantage at any given moment. He didn't need to
confess secrets to a woman like that.

'No one, ma'am. Just ain't anything I would do.'

She pulled up her top, a look crossing her face that said
she felt suddenly embarrassed at her nakedness, as if
another woman hidden inside her had taken over, one
who realized the Good Lord gave gifts to a woman she
should save for someone who meant more than a silver
dollar.

'I don't just want you to find the man who took
Chinadoll and did what he did to me, Mr McCoy.' She
didn't look at him, but wrapped her arms about herself
and stared at the ground.

'That's not what you told me a moment ago.'

'I didn't quite tell you the truth. I want you to take me
with you so I can kill him myself.'

'You got no business doing that,' was all he could think
to say and he knew it sounded lame. 'Fact is, I'm already
lookin' for this fella. He kidnapped a railroad man's

daughter and I aim to see her returned. I'll bring your friend back if possible but killin' him is up to me.'

Her head lifted, surprise and a measure of relief on her features. 'You ain't lost nothin' to this man, Mr McCoy. I have. I should be the one to make him pay.'

'It's a job for a professional manhunter, not a girl. Killin' a man ain't somethin' that leaves you be; it haunts you all your life, even if he deserves that killin'. I don't want that on your conscience.'

Her face grew serious, resolved. 'I ain't goin' back. Whether you take me with you or not I'll be behind you every step of the way. I got nothin' back in Danton.'

He sighed, seeing the determination in her eyes and knowing he wouldn't change her mind. He reckoned that left him little choice. Tracking men such as these was dangerous business and if she came stumbling along behind him she might get them both killed. He would agree to her demands until he figured out a way to get rid of her.

Going to his saddle-bags, which lay in the sand near the fire, he pulled out a stick of jerky. After handing it to her, he poured her a cup of coffee from the blue-enameled pot resting on a rock.

She lowered herself to the ground cross-legged, the folds of her skirt rising and showing a good measure of ankle. He tried not to look but, hell, was a peek such a trespass, considering what she had shown him a few minutes ago?

She remained silent, finishing her coffee while he busied himself with unsaddling her horse, which was a whey-bellied mule of a creature and a sad excuse for a mount.

After eating, she gained her feet and walked to the stream to rinse out the cup, then stood staring out at the diamonds of moonlight sparkling from the water.

Wrapping her arms about herself, the cup dangling from one finger, she stood there for long moments. Trace wondered what was going through her thoughts, betting he knew. His rebuff had likely been her first and she was probably working on a powerful dislike for him. While he couldn't claim to be an expert on the fair sex he reckoned women in general and doves in particular didn't cotton to being rejected; maybe it had something to do with whatever made them become whores in the first place. Whatever the reasoning, it had never been any of his concern and wasn't now. She was just a nuisance.

She came back towards the fire and with a nod he indicated his spread-out bedroll. 'You take the blanket. Nights get right cold this time of year.'

'Reckon colder than they have to be . . .'

He wasn't certain whether he heard sarcasm or disappointment in her voice but wasn't about to ask, either. He dragged his saddle closer to the fire, then sat. He would use it for a pillow and his coat for a cover.

Coralie tucked herself beneath the blanket, drawing it up to her chin, and peered at him. 'Thank you, Mr McCoy.' Her voice came sincere, devoid of any pretense or device.

'Any gentleman would do the same. Like I said, autumn nights have a chill that goes clean to your bones.'

'No, that ain't what I meant. What I offered you . . .' Her gaze dropped and her lips quivered but she quickly regained her composure and met his eyes. 'What I offered, well, most men would have taken it without a second thought. Thank you for refusing.'

He couldn't have been any more surprised if his horse had just walked over and kicked him in the head. His earlier assessment of her thoughts had been dead wrong. He expected anger, perhaps even more hurt and certainly the cold shoulder for the remainder of the trip, but he caught none of that in her tone. She meant what she said, and it told him he didn't know a damn thing about women.

Pulling the blanket up further, she closed her eyes and in that moment, with the glow of the firelight dancing across her face, she looked somehow innocent, despite the warpaint. Her resemblance to Karen struck him again and the notion didn't provide him a lick of comfort. It had taken a good measure of control to turn her down earlier and maybe a fair amount of stupidity. He hadn't been with a woman since Karen's death and had never given it much thought; he'd been too focused on revenge.

He thought about it now, wondered what it would be like to hold her, feel her lips on his, touch her skin.

'Judas Priest,' he whispered, shaking his head. He glanced at her again, deciding she had fallen asleep, which brought a measure of relief. He didn't need her distracting him any more than she had already.

Leaning over, he dragged his saddle-bags near, being as quiet as possible. He turned his back to Coralie and flipped open a flap. Pulling out a rolled Wanted dodger, he felt the rush of anger that always came when he gazed at the likeness sketched on the time-worn poster. A hard face, with black stringy, hair and deep-set dark eyes. A demon face, without compassion, without a soul. John Harrigan: outlaw, killer and all around bastard.

Trace's fingers bleached and trembled with strain as he grasped the edges of the paper tighter.

'I'll find you, you sonofabitch . . .' he whispered.

A gasp from behind startled him from his spell and he turned to see Coralie sitting up, looking over his shoulder.

'That man . . .' Her voice quavered.

'He's a killer, ma'am. I been lookin' for him for an eternity, seems like.'

'He's the one who violated me, Mr McCoy.' Her tone went icy, certain.

'What?' Something cold settled in his belly. 'You sure about that? This ain't no pirate and he ain't been seen for years. He might even be dead.'

Conviction filled her eyes. 'No, he ain't dead. He's the man who took Chinadoll and raped me. He's got a patch now, but I ain't never like to forget that face.'

Disbelief made his brow furrow. 'It's a drawing. Maybe it just looks like—'

'No, that's *him*, I'm tellin' you! He's the bastard who raided the saloon, Mr McCoy, and he's the man I'm going to kill.' The cold fury on her face told him she was convinced of that fact and a chill slid down his spine. Did he dare even to hope she was right? It wasn't likely she would mistake the man after what he'd done to her, but how could a suspected dead outlaw be the same man with an eyepatch and hook leading a band of pirates now?

It made little sense but then Harrigan always had been one stirrup short. Was it possible? he asked himself a second time, unable to deny a surge of hope he wished he didn't feel.

Coralie settled back into her bed and closed her eyes. He gazed at the dodger and found despite himself he desperately wanted to believe her words.

He swung around towards the fire, staring into the flames, lost in the past and lost in hate.

A chance.

When he least expected it. For the hundredth time in five years he said a prayer to his Maker that this time the trail wouldn't end in disappointment.

FIVE

False dawn washed the sky in shades of gray and Trace McCoy sat watching the horizon brighten. He'd slept damn little after Coralie revealed the pirate leader might be John Harrigan. Although exhausted, he was afraid to sleep and invite the nightmare of Karen's death to return. The knowledge, the dim hope, somehow made things too raw, brought the memories too close to the surface.

Was John Harrigan this pirate gang leader who had been plundering towns in this parcel of Colorado? Was he the devil kidnapping innocent women and whores alike?

Trace couldn't make himself accept that as gospel quite yet. Coralie might be dead wrong and to take the word of a distraught—

He caught himself. Had he been about to say *whore?* Did that make a difference? Did it make her identification of the man any less legitimate than that of, say, a reverend's wife?

Of course, it didn't. He was merely looking for ways to soften the blow if the pirate turned out to be someone other than Harrigan.

That's not the only reason you stopped yourself from calling her what she is. The word pricks you now for some reason. Why?

Christamighty, he couldn't figure himself sometimes, but he couldn't deny the notion that the woman sleeping

69

in his bedroll being a lady of the line made something in his belly cinch, even more so in the pre-dawn light. Twenty-four hours ago he wouldn't have given a damn. But since meeting her. . .

Since meeting her, what, McCoy? What's different now?

He glanced at Coralie, who had tossed and turned the entire night. He reckoned she had her own nightmares to contend with. At times he had stifled the urge to wake her from whatever plagued her sleeping thoughts, perhaps as much out of some selfish need for her company as to rescue her from subconscious terrors. The realization puzzled him nearly as much as his nascent qualms about her profession. What business was it of his? He didn't care about her and her life choices and personal demons were her problem.

The fire had died to snapping embers and he downed a cup of cold coffee. Going to the stream, he knelt, splashing water on to his face and toweling off on a sleeve. Bitterly cold, the water stung his skin and sent a shiver down his spine.

A sound came from behind him and he stood, turning to see Coralie sitting up and rubbing sleep from her eyes. She wrapped the blanket around her shoulders, gazed at him, then away, face unreadable. He gathered twigs and loose branches and got the fire restarted, then made a fresh pot of coffee. The rising sun splashed the sky with yellow, gold and orange. Fall leaves glistened with melting frost that dripped in sparking liquid topaz.

After finishing her coffee, Coralie went to the stream and splashed water on her face, shivering the entire time. She knelt there for long moments and he wondered what she was doing. When she stood, she dried her face with the folds of her skirt. As she turned to him, he saw she had scrubbed most of the warpaint from her face. She looked years younger somehow, except for deeper lines about her eyes and mouth, lines that betrayed a life of hardship and trial. Those creases made her look no less attractive; in fact they accorded her a beauty that made her resemble Karen more than he cared to admit. He struggled against a sudden desire to caress her face, her hair, her . . .

What the devil's wrong with you, McCoy? You ain't thought that way about a woman in five years and now's a piss-poor time to start, especially with a woman like that.

Shaking his head, he went to the horses before the impulse grew any stronger and saddled them up. While she rinsed the cup and coffee-pot, he kicked out the fire. He untethered his mount and climbed into the saddle. She tucked the cup and pot into his saddle-bags then followed his direction, mounting her own horse, guiding it up the rise and on to the trail.

Forced into a slower pace than he would have set on his own, he figured they would reach Lazarette by late afternoon. Coralie was no horsewoman and the mount the livery man had palmed off on her was a second-rate glue built for comfort rather than speed.

Trace pondered what they would find when they reached Lazarette. Had the gang hit that town? Was there a possibility of catching them in the act? Hell, the more time it took getting there the more remote that prospect became. He caught himself wishing he had left camp before Coralie awoke; he could have been in Lazarette by now. At the same time a dissenting voice in his mind told him he preferred her company to being alone.

'That man on your poster . . .' Her voice came low and she kept her gaze focused straight ahead.

'What about him?'

'What's his name?'

He swallowed against a knot of emotion tightening his throat. 'John Harrigan.'

'Why'd you think he was dead?'

He shrugged. 'He ain't been seen in years. Rumor has it he just vanished, killed by Indians or some such.'

'You been after him a long spell?'

'Like I said, an eternity seems like.'

She glanced at him. 'Call me Coralie.'

'That your real name?'

She uttered a wispy laugh. 'It's as good as any. Coralie Duvalier. When I was young I wanted to be one of them fancy French ladies. Reckon a name's as close to it as I'll get.' She paused. 'You think it's a pretty name?'

The question caught him off guard and his discomfort increased. 'Does it matter what I think?'

She cast him an annoyed look. 'What the hell kind of answer is that, Mr McCoy?'

Damned if he knew. Fact was, he had no idea why he had said it, unless it was an excuse to avoid revealing that anything about her was attractive to him. She was a whore and men didn't tell whores the things they told lovers or wives. Which made him all the more surprised when he said: 'Reckon it's a pretty name.' A reluctant note hung in his voice and he knew her name wasn't the only thing about her he found enticing. She continued peering at him another moment, then turned her attention back to the trail.

'Why you looking for him?'

'He's wanted for murder.'

'Someone payin' you to find him?'

His belly cinched. 'No, can't say anyone is.'

'You got personal reasons?'

'Reckon that's as good a way to put it as any.' He noticed his palms were damp and tightened his grip on the reins.

'You're a strange man, Mr McCoy, you know that?'

'I'm aware of the fact.'

She let out a clipped laugh. 'I mean, you hunt down

men and kill them, and folks pay you to do it.'

'I'd be the first to admit it's not the most honorable profession but it's far too late to have second thoughts.'

She shook her head. 'It's more than that. There's somethin' else that makes you do it.'

'Don't know what you mean.'

'You got a hell of a reason for spending so long lookin' for this man, I figure. You want him dead and won't rest till he is.'

'Ain't that what you want?' he countered, a heavy note of defensiveness lacing his tone. He felt right annoyed at her prying, not so much because it was none of her business, which it wasn't, but because it made him feel somehow closer to her, made him feel he had to explain his motivations and appear something he was not in her eyes. A foolish notion, but he couldn't force it away.

'This woman you mentioned last night, the one whose memory you keep . . . you love her?'

The question stung and he ran his tongue over dry lips. 'Yeah, reckon that might even be a mild word for it.'

'Always wondered how it would feel to have a fella love me that way. Wondered how it would feel to really love him back.'

At a loss for words, he didn't dare look over at her and kept his gaze locked on the trail. The sun splashed wavering amber light across the hardpack, cavorting with dancing shadows from the forest that lined either side. Boughs interlaced overhead in an emerald canopy, broken only by the flame-gold leaves quaking aspens interspersed amongst the evergreen. Leaves, dry and brittle, fluttered loose occasionally, drifting to the ground, and cracked beneath the horses' hoofs. It all appeared so peaceful against the dark background of his thoughts, making him long for the times he and Karen had taken walks along the stream in autumn. He recollected her kicking up leaves, throwing handfuls of them at him, laughing, running away until he caught her and they rolled on the ground . . .

'Mr McCoy?'

Coralie's voice penetrated his reverie and shook off the thoughts, a strange haunting after-sense of heartache gripping him. He hadn't wanted to drift back to those memory-laced times, invite the crushing grief and lonesomeness, the pain, but sometimes he just couldn't stop himself. He turned to see her peering over at him and knew this time he had slipped, let something from the past show on his face.

'She's dead, ain't she?' Although she said it gently, it felt like a branding iron of grief searing into his soul.

'Yes, she's dead.'

'I'm sorry, Mr McCoy. I truly am.'

'Ain't your concern.'

She shrugged, looking back at the trail. 'This man you're after, he killed her, didn't he?'

His voice dropped and his hands squeezed the reins until his fingers bleached. 'Yes, he did.'

'And now you want to kill him.'

He nodded, afraid his voice would betray him by breaking with emotion.

'What will you do after you kill him?'

He glanced at her, saw the hard set of her features. 'Reckon I don't understand what you're askin'.'

'What do you do after you find this man and kill him? After you got nothing left to make you go on?' Her voice carried a hard edge, as serious as any he had ever heard.

'I can't tell you that.'

'You don't want to?'

'No, because I don't know.' A sigh escaped his lips. With as much as she knew he saw no harm in telling her the rest. Hell, maybe he had wanted to all along. 'I've lived with the thought of finding him all these years. Ain't been room for nothing else and once that's gone I don't think I got a reason to live. Delivering justice has consumed every waking moment. No life beyond that, not for me.'

'You can't just stop livin', Mr McCoy. You just go forward, stumblin' through your life wishin' things weren't the way they are. I want to kill this fella, too. I want to get Chinadoll back alive so she can make her own choices about what she wants, though I rightly don't know what I got to go back to after that. Still don't change the fact that I'll go on livin'. Shouldn't for you, neither.'

What the hell do you know about it? he wanted to snap, but restrained himself. She hadn't lost someone close, hadn't seen a loved one murdered, hadn't chased a ghost over the black nights of endless years.

He was being too hard on her. God knew what trials she'd suffered. She didn't deserve his bitterness any more than Chadburn. He drew a deep breath, reining in his anger.

'What made you the way you are, Miss Coralie?' He asked it before he could stop himself, both out of a sudden need to shift the subject and genuine desire to know more about her. 'What turns a woman into someone who can sell herself for so little?'

She uttered a vapid laugh. 'My ma was a whore, Mr McCoy. A drunk, too. That's pretty much all I recollect about her because she wasn't around most of the time and when she was, she was either passed out or beatin' me, or havin' men in her bed. My pa died when I was four and I barely recollect him, though if I got me an ounce of good it's because of him.'

'You got more than an ounce, I reckon. Most women like you wouldn't bother trying to find a friend.'

'Chinadoll ain't really no one's friend. I reckon most whores don't let themselves get close enough to anyone or each other to set a meanin' to that word. Likely she'd be the first one to tell you I was a damned fool for comin' after her, but I figure she's got some good in her and I aim to give her the chance to find it. Reckon everyone's got some good somewhere if you look deep enough.'

'Not everyone.' His voice came icy, laced with cynicism.

She gazed at him. 'This man we're after, he ain't got no good in him, does he?'

'Reckon if he ever did it's long since rotted away.'

'You think we'll find him in Lazarette?'

'No guarantees, but from what I figure he's headed south and strikes within a fifty-mile radius of this area.'

Her voice dropped and she tensed. 'You reckon we'll find that man's daughter and Chinadoll?'

'Your guess is as good as mine. Don't know what he's doin' with them women but none have showed up and that's damned peculiar. Might mean there's a chance they're alive.' He said it more to give her a measure of reassurance than out of any real belief he would find the woman alive. He knew first-hand what a man like Harrigan could do and that made those women's chances bleak indeed.

She went silent and he sank back into his thoughts. Contemplating the story she had told him, he wondered if she could ever be anything but what she was, at the same time scolding himself for thinking such thoughts. Why had he even let such a notion enter his mind? A whore never changed, no matter how often a body read it in those dime novels. The whore with the heart of gold was a cliché set down by writers with overactive imaginations and this was reality. What the hell did he care, anyway? If they encountered Harrigan in Lazarette neither of them might survive; if they killed the outlaw the same might hold true, at least for him. He had nothing beyond vengeance and that was that.

The morning drifted into afternoon. The day had

warmed but inside Trace McCoy felt only coldness. Coralie grew sullen, dark thoughts reflected on her face, jaw clenched. He reckoned she was thinking of finding the man who had taken something undefinable from her, killing him. She had every right to want him dead but he would see to it the finger on the trigger wasn't hers. If this outlaw leader was indeed Harrigan, he would selfishly never give up the right to put the bullet into the sonofabitch. At the same time, through some strange sense of compassion, he intended to protect her from the guilt that came with killing a man. He wagered she wouldn't likely appreciate it, but that was just too bad.

Lazarette came into view, a small town, its main street wide and rutted. Shiplap buildings with false fronts lined the thoroughfare. Fading sunlight glittered from troughs and windows and the scent of manure and dust filled his nostrils.

He slowed the horse, Coralie following suit, as they entered the town, gaze alert for any sign of trouble. Unlike Danton, all seemed peaceful. Folks shuffled along the boardwalks, going about their business as if they didn't have a care. The serenity ignited selfish disappointment. It was obvious the gang hadn't been here. Did that mean Harrigan and his gang had simply disappeared into the West again? Would finding the bastard prove simply another ghost of the morning? Christ, he was looking for defeat before it happened. There might be a bright side to the fact. If the gang hadn't raided Lazarette, perhaps that meant they would strike later. In that case, Trace McCoy would be here to welcome them. With lead.

He glanced at Coralie. 'We best check in with the local law. Maybe the marshal can point us somewhere.'

She nodded and he wondered if he could somehow find a way to leave her behind, but the chances of that happening seemed to be evaporating. To his surprise, he

was forced to admit the prospect of disentangling himself
from her company didn't appear half as inviting as it had
when she rode into his camp last night.

Reaching the office, they dismounted, tethering the
mounts to the hitch rail. He dug in his saddle-bags for the
Wanted dodger and stuffed it into a pocket. As he went to
the door, he paused, Coralie coming up behind him. He
gave her a once-over, frowning at her torn bodice and
skirt. 'Reckon we best get you some decent clothes after
we see the marshal.'

'Afraid I look too much like a whore, Mr McCoy?' Her
voice sang with a sarcastic lilt that got under his skin.

'Didn't say that.'

She uttered a brittle laugh. 'Ain't got the money to pay
for them, Mr McCoy, and you don't ... barter ...'
Something mischievous in her eyes made him want to
squirm.

'Reckon you can find some other way to repay me
someday.' He stepped into the office before she took a
notion to respond.

A wiry man looked up from behind his desk, on which
he had spread out a newspaper. A foul-smelling stogie
hung from thin lips and filled the entire office with a
cloud of yellowish smoke. His small eyes settled on Trace
with annoyance. He set the cigar on a glass ashtray made
out of the bottom of a whiskey bottle. With small eyes that
brought to mind a chameleon, the marshal surveyed
Coralie.

'You a whore?' The lawdog's lack of tact annoyed Trace
but Coralie's face remained indifferent, though a slight
narrowing of her eyes indicated her indignation.

Ignoring the remark, Trace closed the door behind
them. 'Name's Trace McCoy, Marshal.'

The lawdog tensed, swallowed. 'The bounty man? What
the hell you doin' in Lazarette?' A note of challenge hung

in the man's tone. Trace wasn't sure whether it came in response to the reputation manhunters got tagged with oftentimes or something more significant. Many viewed Trace's ilk as hired killers, without morals or redeeming value. Local law often saw it as an infringement on their territory and an indictment on their ability to produce results. Whatever the case here, the marshal's hackles were raised. Trace would have preferred co-operation instead of confrontation, but the man's rude assessment of Coralie had given him an automatic dislike for the lawdog.

Going to the marshal's desk, Trace pulled out the Wanted dodger and snapped it open, tossing it atop the newspaper. 'You seen this man?'

The marshal picked up the poster, a peculiar look Trace couldn't read crossing his eyes.

'Ain't never seen him, McCoy. Why don't you try lookin' in another town for him?' The marshal tossed the dodger atop the desk and Trace cared little for the man's less than subtle suggestion.

'Had a notion he was headed this way. You ain't had any trouble in this town?'

'What kind of trouble?'

'Looting, any women kidnapped?'

'Hell, no! We run a peaceful town here, McCoy. We got no need for the likes of you.' The man's scrawny chest lifted and the note of antagonism in his tone made Trace think it went beyond the fact the marshal was being territorial. Something else had lit his lamp; Trace wondered just what it was.

'You know anything 'bout that pirate gang seen in the area?' He studied the lawman's face and a flicker of recognition might have registered in his eyes but the lawdog concealed it too fast for Trace to be certain.

'Pirates, Mr McCoy? Ain't an ocean in miles of here. Maybe you done came to the wrong place after all.' He smiled, as if that diluted the sarcasm in his words, but in fact it only augmented Trace's growing urge to wipe the smug attitude off his face.

'You must have heard about them, Marshal,' Coralie put in. 'They been takin' young women all around these parts.'

The marshal kept his gaze focused on Trace and a sly smile crossed his lips. 'One of the perks of bein' a famous fella like yourself gettin' your choice of whores to travel with, McCoy?'

Trace's dislike for the man deepened. He battled an urge to take a swing at the lawdog, knowing it wouldn't help the situation any, but it was all he could do to hold back. His eyes narrowed as he studied the man's face, trying to peg his character and a moment later he reckoned he had it: the marshal was a man who relished whatever power his position gave him and wielded it without restraint over those he believed below him. Demeaning a whore was an easy mark. Trace had seen his type before and they all came with a streak of cowardice and a penchant for back-shooting.

Scarlet colored Coralie's face and she gave the lawdog a look of unbridled spite. 'What I am ain't no concern of yours, Marshal.'

The lawdog met her gaze this time and his face darkened. 'Everything in this town's my concern, missy, whether it's some whore thinkin' she can back-talk me or some manhunter lookin' to create a problem where none exists. You best keep a civil tongue, 'less you want trouble.' His gaze swung to Trace. 'And you, McCoy, you just keep in mind Lazarette is a peaceful town and it damn well better stay that way. Your type ain't needed or welcome here and I reckon it'd be best if you considered movin' on soon.'

Trace nodded, refusing to let the man make him lose

his composure. He scooped up the Wanted poster and tucked it into his pocket, keeping his eyes locked on the marshal. 'I aim to find this man. And I aim to stop him from taking girls and robbing saloons.' He cocked an eyebrow. 'I'd expect you'd have that same interest, seeing you're a lawman.'

'Like I said, I ain't seen the man on your dodger, McCoy. Reckon he high-tailed it for parts unknown.'

Trace looked at Coralie, who appeared on the verge of giving the lawman a piece of her mind, but was likely holding her tongue because she knew nothing would be served by causing a commotion.

Going to the door and opening it, Trace tipped a finger to his hat. 'You got a hotel in this town, Marshal?'

The lawdog's face hardened. 'You got sand in your ears, McCoy?'

'I heard you just fine, Marshal. But I reckon we'll stay a short spell anyway. Been on the trail a while and this town seems like a right fine place to rest up.' Trace nodded to Coralie, who stepped outside. He shut the door behind them.

On the boardwalk, he peered at the young woman. 'Reckon you could have said a lot in there, way he treated you.'

'Ain't worth it. I seen his type enough. What he says don't matter none to me. Most folks don't think too highly of whores, even the men who use them.' Sadness crossing her face, she went to her horse, untethering the reins, then stepping into the saddle. Whore with a heart of gold, those dime novels said. Trace reckoned they were wrong, at least for Coralie. Her heart was likely made of something a whole lot more fragile.

SIX

After Trace McCoy departed, Marshal Clyde Trainor sat staring at the door, irritation sending a prickly sensation through the hairs on the back of his neck, suspicion welling in his mind. A man like that riding into Lazarette could mean nothing but trouble, and since he had come looking for pirate gangs that trouble wouldn't be long in coming.

From everything Trainor had read, McCoy was a ruthless bastard and he rarely failed to get his man. More hardcases than not never saw the inside of a courtroom; many wound up with a hemp necktie or lead pill. The marshal ran a finger over his upper lip, wondering just how much chance McCoy stood of finding Morgan, and, more importantly, whether the trail would lead right back to this office. He couldn't have that, no sirree. He had grown far too accustomed to living.

He contemplated that gal with McCoy. What the hell was a fella like that doin' travelin' with a bargirl? Made no sense, unless Morgan had done something to her, or perhaps had taken one of the woman's friends. Them gals weren't known as the most charitable of souls, but you never knew. He reckoned it didn't matter a hell of a lot anyway, because the manhunter was staying in town and if he happened to spot DeFete entering this office there'd be hell to pay.

He uttered an ironic laugh, making a mental note to have an escape plan in ready. Bardoves might not be the most loyal of sorts, but neither were lawmen with their hand in the till.

Another particular surfaced in Trainor's mind: that Wanted poster . . . the man on it looked downright familiar. Fact, he looked a hell of a lot like DeFete. But his name was what? Harrigan, John Harrigan. That was it. Wanted for murder. Was McCoy on the trail of two men or was the outlaw in that poster. . . ?

A clank sounded at the back of the room, near the stairs leading to the upper level where Trainor kept a room. He started, gaze jumping to the rear door, which was opening in cautious increments. His belly plunged as a man stepped into the office, a man who might have been Old Nick himself for all he was concerned, and for the briefest of moments he panicked that Devil had somehow overheard his mutinous thoughts and come to kill him.

'What are you doin' in town?' he blurted, half-rising from his chair.

The man eased the door shut. 'Why are you so all-fired jittery, matey? You should have been expectin' me to ride in after the last couple raids.'

Morgan DeFete stepped deeper into the room and Trainor collapsed back into his seat. He scolded himself for showing fear. He hated the streak of cowardice he exhibited whenever in DeFete's presence. But, hell and damnation, the man was as like to shoot his own men as his enemies.

'A man was here, lookin' for you, is all. Made me jumpy.'

As DeFete stopped in front of the desk, the hilt of the sword at his hip gleamed in a shaft of late-afternoon sunlight that streamed through the dusty window. 'What man?'

'Said his name was Trace McCoy.'

'The manhunter?' DeFete's face darkened and his one eye roved. That eye gave Trainor the goddamn willies.

'He's no fella to have on your trail, Morgan.'

'Inclined to agree, but let him come.'

'Had a whore with him, too.'

DeFete's brow furrowed. 'What'd this whore look like?'

'Brown hair, in rings that fell over her shoulders, blue bodice.'

Morgan's gaze drifted off, as if deep in thought. 'Hell, I seen so many whores that don't mean much. She say what she wanted?'

'No, but McCoy said he was lookin' for the pirate gang that's been takin' gals 'round these parts.'

'Wonder if that explains why Crawford ain't come back yet.'

'You reckon McCoy got him?'

'Be my guess. Hell, he was a waste anyhow. Would have just made him walk the plank sooner or later.'

Trainor shuddered, knowing full well what that meant and not caring for the images it invoked. 'You think McCoy just took a notion to take up your trail by himself?'

Morgan's gaze shifted to the window. 'Reckon that railroad man hired him. He's the only one who's got the means. No one would come lookin' for whores.'

'I told you that it was a mistake goin' after that blue blood—'

'Did you, now?' Morgan's left arm swept up in a blur of motion and Trainor had no time to get out of the way. The hook tore a gory chasm across his cheek and he let out a bleat of pain. He grabbed at his face and blood streamed between his fingers. Plucking a bandanna from his pocket, he tried to staunch the flow, but it quickly saturated the cloth. 'Holy Christ, why'd you do that, Morgan?'

DeFete slung a leg over the edge of the desk and leaned towards the lawman. 'No one questions my orders, matey. Not my men, and not the likes of you. You best recollect that next time you get a hankering to second-guess me. That gal will fetch a high price, highest yet, most like. She's plumb easy to scare, too.'

Trainor's gaze flicked to the other man. He felt an over-powering urge to bolt from his chair and get as far from the pirate leader's presence as he could, but he knew that would result in certain death. He reckoned DeFete was the only man he felt afeared of and with damned good reason, but the feeling still ate at his innards and he would make sure a whore paid for that tonight. Beatin' the hell out of them always made him feel better.

'T-that McCoy,' Trainor said before DeFete took the notion to strike him again. 'He was lookin' for another fella, too.'

DeFete wiped the blood on his hook across a trouser leg. 'Who?'

'An outlaw named Harrigan.'

Surprise flickered on DeFete's face, vanished. 'John Harrigan . . . Ain't heard that name in a spell.'

'Who is he?'

DeFete's one-eyed gaze fell on Trainor and the marshal winced, despite himself. 'He's no one you'd want to know, Trainor. This McCoy stayin' in town?'

'Asked me if there was a hotel, said he was here for a short spell.'

'You keep an eye on him. He even pisses wrong you let me know about it.'

Marshal Trainor gave a jerky nod and dabbed at his face. The cut wasn't especially deep but it stung like a sonofabitch and bled liberally. He knew Morgan had pulled the blow just enough; if he hadn't, that damn hook would have gone straight through his cheek. He had seen DeFete impale a bargirl with it once and the sight had never traveled far from his nightmares.

When the leader spoke again it came with the effect of a gunshot going off near Trainor's ear and he jolted. 'This McCoy, describe him.'

The marshal sketched a word picture of the manhunter and DeFete appeared to grapple with some memory, the look in his eye growing distant.

'Mean anything to you?' The question came tentative and Trainor tensed for a possible explosive reaction.

'Hell, somethin' about him sounds familiar, but I can't rightly place it. Maybe it's just what I heard about him.'

The marshal remained silent, the stinging slash on his face a constant reminder the man might kill him with little provocation. A passing thought made him almost wish McCoy would string up the gang leader and release him from the prison of his fear, but then the percentage he got for his part in the operation would dry up as well.

'I got four gals and one extra I ain't sure about,' said Morgan, breaking the silence.

'I got buyers for 'em, down Mexico way. They're ridin' up to finish the transaction. They'll pay big money for that man's daughter, way you said. Couple of bigwig chili-eaters lookin' for wives, young pretty ones. But they want five, maybe more.'

Morgan nodded. 'I got four for sure. They're practically pissin' themselves they're so afeared I'm gonna kill 'em. But I got this chink with a right big mouth. She's gettin' under my skin and I ain't sure she can be broke. I'll find me a couple extra as back-ups.'

Trainor gave a jerky nod. 'Best not attract McCoy's attention doin' it . . .'

Morgan stood and took a step away from the desk. 'Don't you worry 'bout that none, matey. Man's plumb loco comin' after me, but if he wants trouble I'll give it to him.' DeFete whirled, swinging his hook a second time. Trainor let out a bleat and pressed his eyes shut, waiting to feel the cold metal slice through his face. The hook swished through the air and thunked into the desktop, shredding the newspaper and gouging a deep crevice into the wood.

With a clipped laugh, Morgan DeFete strode towards the rear door. Trainor chanced opening his eyes. Sweat beaded on his forehead and poured down his face, mixing with the blood running from the slice across his cheek.

'You best get some balls you want to keep workin' for me, Trainor. Reckon I ain't particularly sure I can rely on cowards.'

The marshal nodded, afraid to say anything that would worsen the situation. Morgan stepped out of the office and for an eternity after he left Trainor didn't move, petrified, and blessed with the uncomfortable knowledge he had pissed himself with the last swing of that hook.

'Don't s'pose that's your wife?' The hotel man gave Trace a raised eyebrow, but snapped up the greenbacks the manhunter slid across the counter. Without waiting for the answer, the clerk turned the ledger towards Trace, who signed his name.

Coralie's face brightened with a mischievous expression. 'Why, yes, sir, I'm the lady McCoy. We just got hitched yesterday.' She appeared suddenly very innocent and demure, and Trace might have laughed under other circumstances. She grinned, clutching tightly to a brown-paper-wrapped package tucked beneath an arm. Ever since walking out of the dress shop, where he'd purchased a less conspicuous garment she'd picked out, along with whatever the hell it was womenfolk wore beneath their clothes, she'd clung to the bundle like a little girl with a new doll.

The hotel man blew out a dubious sigh. 'Reckon it ain't rightly none of my business anyhow.'

Coralie giggled, but her tone carried an edge that told Trace she was wearying of folks treating her a certain way for what she was. Maybe that was a good sign.

Trace slid the ledger across the counter and took the key the man offered.

'Upstairs, third door to the right.' The clerk ducked his chin towards the stairs.

Trace grabbed his saddle-bags from the countertop and headed for the stairs. Coralie gave the hotel man a wink and hurried after the manhunter.

Once in the room, the young woman tore open the package like it was her first Christmas and held up a simple blue cotton dress with a row of shot stitched into the bottom of the breadths to make riding that nag of hers a bit more practical. She gave him a look and he frowned, turning away as she dressed.

'You develop a sudden case of the bashfuls?' He asked it half in jest, but perhaps with more hope than he cared to admit.

'That the type of woman you want me to be?' Something in her tone sent a peculiar flutter through his belly.

'You best be the type of woman you got inside. What other folks want don't matter.'

'I'm used to lyin', Mr McCoy. I've spent years practicing. Men want me to act a certain way so I play the part. I've learned to abide with it, but sometimes I ain't sure who I really am no more.'

The sorrow in her voice made him turn and a small gasp escaped his lips. The dress fitted snugly at her waist and flaring hips and stretched taut across the bosom in a way he wasn't the least bit comfortable with. With the high-buttoned collar she looked like a church-going woman to be courted by any cowboy this side of the Rockies. Truth be told, he found her quite lovely and it took him a moment to get his breath back.

'We all got choices to make . . .' His voice came low, a bit unsteady. 'We make lot of wrong ones but maybe they ain't all permanent. Reckon you could choose to be who you really are.'

She looked at the floor, back to him. 'Might say the same about yourself, Mr McCoy.'

He uttered a scoffing laugh. 'I ain't got no more choices. They were taken from me five years ago.'

Sympathy bled into her eyes and he reckoned it was genuine. In a way he didn't understand, he liked it there, perhaps even needed it from her in that moment. She wasn't as hard as she wanted folks to believe.

'After you find this man, Mr McCoy, you might have choices again . . .' Her voice was nearly inaudible, tentative.

'Don't know what you mean.'

Averting her gaze, she appeared on the verge of saying something more, but whatever it was remained unspoken. She gestured to the bed. 'We both sleeping on that?' No coyness this time; instead, something almost innocent and pure, as if she were trying to explore what it was like to be a woman of morals and breeding.

He almost smiled. 'You take the bed. I'll sleep in the chair. I prefer that anyway.'

She nodded and lowered herself on to the edge of the mattress, shoulders slumping, exhaustion likely catching up to her. He reckoned she had been running on emotion the past couple days and her reserves had bottomed out. So had his and he wasn't quite sure what kept him going on so little sleep, but if he stopped now he would likely collapse. He couldn't allow that, not when he might be close to Harrigan.

He pulled a roll of greenbacks from his pocket and stuffed them into his saddle-bags, then headed for the door. Stopping, he looked back to her. 'You'll need money for supper. Take it out of that roll.'

A surprised look crossed her face. 'You trust me?'

'Don't have to. I trust your need to get this fella who took your friend and doubt you'd know how to do that alone or you wouldn't have come after me.'

It likely wasn't quite the answer she wanted if the look in her eyes was any indication, but she nodded. 'Where are you goin'?'

'Gonna ask around a bit, see if anyone at the saloon or on the street has any lead to the gang. Gonna pay that marshal another visit, too. Somethin' 'bout the way he was actin' strikes me suspicious as hell.'

'He was lyin'.' She said it as if it were gospel.

He nodded, knowing if anyone was a judge of a man's character she likely was an expert. 'You stay here and rest a bit. I'll let you know if I find anything.'

'That a promise, Mr McCoy? I'm inclined to take the word of a man like yourself.'

He almost warned her not to be gullible, even with a man like him, but thought better of it. She didn't seem disposed to arguing about accompanying him and he preferred to keep it that way. She wasn't the naïve type anyway.

'You can take my word on it.' He turned to leave.

'Mr McCoy . . .' A measure of concern laced her voice.

He paused, hand on the knob. 'Yeah?'

'Be careful . . . please?'

'Always am.' He reckoned it wasn't the last lie he would tell her.

She gave him a thin laugh. 'No, you're not.'

He glanced at the floor, looked back to her. She was right: sometimes he wasn't careful at all. Sometimes it was just easier to walk into hell than let the Devil catch up with you.

'I'll have the hotel man send a bath up while I'm gone. I'll give you a couple hours.'

Her eyes brightened. 'Thank you, Mr McCoy. Thank you for treating me . . . like a lady.'

'Never a question of that in my mind.'

He headed for the stairs, wondering if she had been treated decently by a man since her father died. He doubted it and the notion unsettled him. Perhaps if her life had been different she might have been more like Karen, or Chadburn's daughter. He wondered sometimes why things happened the way they did, why Fate threw some folks from the saddle and gave others less deserving a smooth ride.

It was that way with him and Karen. Karen did not deserve what she got. He reckoned a sweeter woman never walked God's green, and for all his faults he hadn't committed any unpardonable sin he could see, none worthy of the punishment those men doled out that day five years ago. It wasn't fair; life wasn't fair and seeing the cards Fate had dealt to Coralie made him all the more disgusted with it.

Christ, why was he thinking on that again? He'd spent a thousand endless nights pondering God's plan only to reach the same conclusion: it made no goddamned sense and never would.

But such ruminations no longer mattered. With all the men he had killed on the trail to Harrigan he had enough black marks in his book to send him straight to hell. And at the moment he didn't care a lick. He doubted he ever would.

SEVEN

Could a man like Trace McCoy ever love a woman like her?

The question lingered in her mind as she slid deeper into the lavender-scented water of the bath the hotel man had brought up. An aching sense of despair welled in her heart, grief for the woman she might have been. The emotion was fleeting, replaced with a burst of unprecedented anger at what she was, a woman who sold her favors and wasn't too powerful particular about whom she sold them to.

It wasn't completely her choice, despite Trace McCoy's words to the contrary. How could she choose to be the woman she wanted to be after the way she was forced to grow up, to survive? She reckoned a time or two a chance to get out had presented itself, but she refused to recognize it, whether from the blind fear of what existed beyond whoring or some deep dark need inside that made her no better than those laudanum-addicted doves who couldn't quit their habit. What skills did she have other than the soft curves with which God furnished a woman? She couldn't sew or cook; she had none of the domestic qualities a fella sought in a wife. Christamighty, she'd never even learned to read and write. She was too busy findin' ways to avoid her ma's drunken wrath for any such learning.

Besides, whoring had come natural after what those men did to her, hadn't it? Lies and soft whispers tumbled from her lips with too familiar intimacy.

Despite the fact her mother's beaux had ripped away her virtue, the first man she had taken by choice left her feeling soiled and humiliated, reduced her to vomiting on to an outhouse floor and shaking for days after. Past the first few times it wasn't so hard, but she reckoned all the baths in the West wouldn't clean all the filth from her soul.

Trace McCoy would never want a woman like her, plain and simple. He loved another, cherished her enough to spend his life tracking down her killer, enough to take no other woman into his bed. He was so unlike the men she encountered in saloons, caring and compassionate, beneath his hard exterior. Dedicated to his woman's memory and a mission of justice in her honor. She wondered what made this woman so special and a certain bitter jealousy filled her being for a person she had never even known. It was unreasonable and selfish, but she couldn't help it. Oh, how she wanted to hate that woman for living in his mind the way she did, but she had no right; it was not that woman's fault. She was dead, murdered by the horrible man who had taken Chinadoll.

Coralie let out a fragile laugh, something inside her breaking down, wanting to consume her with emotion and regret. It wasn't often she let herself cry, but she did now. Tears streamed down her cheeks, dripping into the water like the lost chances of her life diluting in the Devil's ocean of schemes.

She wrapped her arms about herself and sobbed, mind filled with thoughts of Trace McCoy and the man who violated her. While she still wanted that gang leader dead by her hand, she wondered if maybe that desire hadn't weakened. Could she deny Trace the satisfaction of pulling the trigger after what the killer had taken from him? After all, what he stole from her she usually sold for a silver dollar.

The notion struck her that for one of the few times she could recollect the needs of another seemed more important than her own. The feeling confused her, made her wonder why she couldn't get his face out of her thoughts and the jealousy for his lost love out of her mind. She half-wished he had taken what she had to offer at camp last night. It would have made things so much easier, placed him in a category with every other man who ever lay with her. The notion vanished as quickly as it came. That wasn't what she wanted at all.

Tears flowed harder and the question she had asked Trace on the trail suddenly haunted her; what happened after they killed the outlaw? She had asked out of selfishness, though he likely hadn't realized it. She had wanted to know if there would be even the slightest of chances, of hopes, of dreams he might let her stay with him for a spell and maybe . . .

What the hell you doin' even thinkin' that for? she scolded herself. She had no call; that right had been forfeit the first time one of her ma's fellas took her into the barn and set her on the path straight to immorality. But she had never felt anything like the emotions churning inside her now.

'I want you to love me . . .' Her whisper came out before she could stop it. She placed her head in her hands and let the tears flow until the water turned cold and the ice around her heart froze solid again.

Trace McCoy spent a bit over an hour questioning folks on the street and showing them the Wanted poster, but came up empty. No one had seen John Harrigan and no one knew anything about pirate gangs other than rumor. A niggling suspicion made him ponder why the gang hit every town in a line heading south except Lazarette, but perhaps they were lying low after that last raid, waiting to see if any law got on their trail. That appeared to contradict their brazen style, which made him want to discount the notion.

Was he grasping at straws? Maybe. Maybe he wanted Harrigan so bad it clouded his judgment. Still, he couldn't overlook even the most remote possibility. And that meant another visit with the local law, whom he felt certain was hiding something.

He sauntered along the boardwalk, the sun touching the western horizon now, a chill weaving into the air.

Reaching the marshal's office, he stepped inside. The lawdog started and looked at him with wide eyes. Trace was willing to bet his presence had little to do with it. Something had changed about the tin star's manner and Trace tried to determine exactly what.

Fear. Fear had invaded the office and erased some of the cockiness from the marshal's demeanor. He noted a bandage taped across the man's cheek, a splotch of browned blood showing through.

'You have an accident?' Trace saw the marshal's eyes shift back and forth.

'What the hell you doin' back here?'

Trace came towards the desk. Noticing a deep gouge in the top, he wondered whether that had been there on his previous visit but recollected a newspaper had been spread across the top earlier. It appeared fresh and combined with the lawman's dressing it redefined his suspicions. Had the man received a visitor after Trace departed?

'It occurred to me you weren't the most obligin' of sorts when I was here before, Marshal.'

'So? I ain't the goddamn welcomin' committee.' The

man's tone came sharp, attempting to override the fear saddling a hitch to his voice, but failing.

Trace met his gaze. 'What happened to your face?'

The man averted his gaze. 'Cut myself shaving, if it's any goddamn concern of yours.' He said it too fast, as if he had been holding the excuse for just such an exigency.

'Forget to strop your straight edge?' Trace didn't bother concealing the sarcasm in his voice.

'Your concern for my welfare overwhelms me, but that don't change the fact we don't need your type in this town.'

'Don't you?'

'What the hell's that s'posed to mean?'

Trace shrugged. 'Just wondered if this town really is as peaceful as you make it out to be. Maybe you're livin' on the edge of the storm.'

The marshal shifted in his seat, clearly uncomfortable with the question. 'Like I said, we got no need of your type. I'm the law here and I see to things just fine.' The marshal tried to put intensity in his voice but the effort fell short. Something had unhinged him since their last meeting.

'I'm gonna ask you again if you seen that man on my poster, Marshal. And I aim to keep askin' till I get the answer I want.'

The belligerence returned to the lawman's tone. 'Told you, ain't never seen him before. You best take a notion to accept that and ride out 'fore somethin' happens to you.'

Trace eyed him. All pretense dropped, the man had just made a clear threat as far as he was concerned.

'That sounds a hell of a lot like you got your hand in someone's till.'

The marshal reached across the desk and opened the lid on a humidor, selecting a cigar and biting off the tip.

Fishing a lucifer from his pocket, he puffed the stogie to life. 'Do yourself a favor, McCoy, and take some advice. This town will stay peaceful long as you don't cause trouble.'

'Reckon you read me that book already. S'pose I decide to ignore that advice?'

'Like I said, things happen to folks who don't mind their own business.'

'You ain't makin' much attempt to hide the fact there's more goin' on here than you're tellin'. That strikes me like a man who's confident he's got his ass covered.'

The marshal held Trace's gaze and cockiness flooded his manner again. 'Don't bet the lives of innocent folks on this, McCoy. It's a fool's bet.'

'What would I bet, Marshal, a silver dollar or a gold doubloon?'

Trainor's face darkened. 'Get the hell outa here, McCoy.' The cigar clamped between his teeth wagged.

Trace let a smile filter on to his lips and went to the door. 'Nice town you got here, Marshal. Peaceful, just like you say. Reckon I might grow to like it more and more the longer I stay.'

The lawdog plucked the stogie from his mouth. 'You're a damned fool, McCoy. You ain't got a clue what you're up against. You did, you'd ride on out with your tail 'twixt your legs.'

A somber look tightened Trace's features. 'Reckon this town's got one lapdog too many as it is . . .'

The lawdog's gaze locked on Trace, a seething threat behind it now. 'I've said all I intend to say.'

'In that case, one other thing, Marshal.'

'What's that, McCoy?'

'I reckon you owe my friend an apology for the way you treated her earlier.'

'You want me to apologize to a whore? You gotta be

plumb loco!' The marshal let out a guffaw and Trace's nerves cinched.

His expression remained darkly serious. 'If it's the last thing you do, Marshal, you'll apologize to her; mark my words.'

'You got a hell of an imagination, McCoy. A hell of an imagination.'

'We'll see about that, Marshal.'

After leaving the office, Trace lingered downsteet about twenty yards, in case the lawman decided to high-tail it and inform whoever was pulling his strings about their conversation. Leaning against a building wall, arms crossed, he felt certain of one thing: the marshal was up to his neck in something and had as much as told him so.

Did it involve Harrigan? If that were the case, Trace hoped to trail the man if he left to meet with the gang leader. Course, the lawman might not come out the front way. While inside, Trace had noted a back door. He wasn't in position to observe that exit, though he reckoned anyone departing that way would have to come out of the alleyway beside the office, especially if he were going to head to the livery for a horse.

An hour later, he began to wonder. Either the marshal wasn't about to carry a message to anyone until he was damn sure it was safe or he was working on his own. Trace waited another two hours but saw no sign of the lawdog.

Patience worn thin and exhaustion turning his legs rubbery, he headed back towards the hotel room. Nightfall had filled the street with swaying shadows and the cidery light of hanging lanterns glowed along the boardwalk. The marshal was off the hook for the time being, but Trace vowed to keep a watch on him from now on.

By the time he reached the room, he discovered Coralie fast asleep beneath the covers. A low-turned lantern sat on the nightstand and in the gloom he stood looking at her face, captured by the way flame-glow and slumber softened her features. She looked much more like Karen now, peaceful, innocent.

Help me . . .

A haunted sensation washing over him, he forced himself to turn away. He went to the lantern, extinguished the flame, then settled into the overstuffed chair, which he pushed into the corner. The moon cast a wan glow through the windows and the breeze made shushing sounds against the shiplap siding. He grew aware of other innocuous sounds, the beating of his heart, the rhythm of Coralie's breathing. He wondered if this was the first time she had slept in a man's room without sharing her bed. The notion of her with many men suddenly made his belly hitch and he reckoned that was a puzzle.

She's a whore.

The more that word forced itself into his mind the more he hated it. An afterthought, telling the marshal he would apologize for calling her that; Trace hadn't planned on saying it. Hell, what had possessed him to defend a bar dove's honor anyway?

Confusion gripping him, he shoved the thoughts away, blaming them on exhaustion. The room began to shimmer and his eyelids grew heavy. His breathing grew regular, deep.

Daylight flashed through his mind and he was no longer in the hotel room. Around him trees rose up, blazing with fall colors. To the left the stream bubbled over rocks, water glittering with jewels of sunlight. The scene appeared hazy, glowing, as if he were viewing the world through frosted glass.

A hand squeezed his fingers and he turned to see the expectation and love shining from Karen's face. Long chestnut hair cascaded over her shoulders, and she wore a simple dress of yellow gingham. All the emotions of that day cascaded through him, hope and happiness, the blinding sense of false security that only comes to young lovers. In his pocket he felt the bulge of a small box holding a ring he would give her when he asked her to marry him in only a few moments.

That chance never came. It hadn't then and it wouldn't now, because Fate chiseled the outcome in granite.

The smile on her face vanished, replaced by a silent scream and look of terror. Blood streamed over her features and he felt her hand wrenched from his. He reached for her, struggled to prevent the events from occurring the way they had a thousand times over, but there was no changing what had been.

At the corners of his vision, men stepped from the forest, six hard men led by a beard-stubbled maniac whose dark eyes showed neither mercy nor anything the slightest bit human. Simply a matter of being in the wrong place at the wrong time, but so much more in the course of two innocent lives.

The hardcase leader grabbed Karen, pulling her back, while the rest of the bandits prevented Trace from going to her aid.

'Nooo, don't hurt her!' His scream met with harsh laughter. He struggled to break their grip, kicking at shins and slamming his forehead into one of the men's faces, who screeched and clutched at his nose while blood poured between his fingers. Another man buried a fist in Trace's belly and he doubled over, retching.

Help me!

Her words rang in his ears and he fought to right himself, go to her, but a man slammed a fist into his temple, stunning him and the world about him spun.

As he collapsed, two bandits grabbed his arms and held him upright, forcing him to watch while the leader took

Karen, then put a bullet through her skull.

He got no time to dwell on the horror of her death, because men began pounding at his face and body. Blow after blow, until he could barely feel their fists or his pain. Somehow he remained unmercifully conscious. When it was over they hurled him to the ground, kicking him for good measure. Another found the ring box in his pocket and tossed it to the leader.

The hardcase grinned and knelt before him, a fist-sized stone in his hand. 'The name's John Harrigan, boy. You recollect that in Hell.' The leader swung the stone, the blow opening a gaping slice on his jaw, and everything went black.

He never knew how or why he lived through the ordeal. When he awoke, Karen lay dead and by all rights he should have perished with her. Christ, so many times he wished he had.

But he recovered, at least physically, broken ribs and jawbone healing, while grief remained an open bleeding wound. Recovered only to be tormented by the fact every-thing he ever wanted and dreamed had been torn away and replaced with a driving compulsion to avenge her death and kill John Harrigan.

He awoke with a gasp, sitting bolt upright. Heart slam-ming against his ribs, sweat pouring from his face and down his chest, he drew shallow breaths, fighting to regain his composure. Trembling, he put his face in his hands.

A hand touched his shoulder and he looked up. Eyes blurry, he struggled to focus. In the moonglow he saw Coralie, dressed in the underthings he'd bought her, peer-ing at him.

'Sorry I woke you,' was all he could say, trying to keep the pain from his voice.

She eased on to his lap and held her finger to his lips. 'Shhh, you don't have to say anything.' Her voice came out a comforting whisper. Withdrawing her finger, she gently kissed his lips, then lay her head against his chest. He wrapped his arms around her, thankful for the comfort she offered, aware of the soft scent of lavender in her hair and gentle beating of her heart.

EIGHT

Dawn splashed gory streaks of light across the sky and bathed the heart of the box canyon in blood and shadow. Glittering ruby water filled the stream that meandered through its center. Oblong, the canyon drew to a point at its southern tip; its northern mouth consisted of a flattened opening a hundred yards across, prompting some long-forgotten prospector to label it the Galleon Canyon, a name that suited Morgan DeFete just fine.

The Buccaneer gang's camp lay within its sheltering confines, its rock walls rising a hundred and fifty feet straight up on either side. The grounds, littered with stunted pine and cottonwood, boulders and deadfalls, scalloped upwards towards the north, affording them protection and advantage should a posse ever foolishly decide to track them here. A fire burned, flames snapping in the chilled morning air. Three men huddled around its heat, gulping coffee and smoking, while two others patrolled the canyon entrance.

The sun climbed higher, gilding the sky and turning the stream waters to shivering amber. Within the center of the stream stood a huge platform ten feet above the surface. Constructed of rough-hewn planks and perched atop logs driven deep into the stream bed, it was erected in the fashion of a two-masted brigantine. Its deck boasted a length of fifty feet and from its front jutted a rapierlike bowsprit. A skull and crossbones flag fluttered in the breeze. Coils of rope and piles of netting lay about and a three-foot-high rail encircled the structure, broken only by a two-foot-wide opening from which protruded a thick plank. To the right rested a weather-beaten old chest with brass handles, its lid propped open. Within lay a hoard of glittering jewels embedded in bracelets and necklaces, as well as silver dollars and double eagles, bounty from the gang's raids. A sign hung from the side of the ship's deck, the legend bearing the name THE OLD ORCHARD in chiseled letters. An ornate ship's wheel stood near deck center.

Morgan DeFete poised at the ship's wheel, gazing over the five women tied against the rail, wondering if taking that railroad man's daughter had been a miscalculation after all. That was the only reason a famous manhunter would be on his trail that he could see.

No mere railroad detective, Trace McCoy was a man to be reckoned with. Morgan knew little about him but he knew that. Although he had never seen a picture of McCoy, something sounded damn familiar from that no-good lawdog's description. In the dim recesses of his mind, he struggled to recollect, finding the memory elusive. Something from long ago, from a time when he was John Harrigan. . . .

No matter. It would come to him eventually and in the meantime he had stock to tame, ready for buyers. Women needed to be molded into decent wives, through intimidation, fear, threat, whatever it took.

His one-eyed gaze swept over the five, four saloon gals and the ivory-skinned priss daughter of Rutherford Chadburn. For a brief time he had considered killing her and delivering the body to her father in pieces for setting that manhunter on his trail, but that would be foolish. The girl would bring in too much money on the Mexican market and DeFete wasn't one to let spite get in the way of greed. She cowered against the rail, trembling, her face shades paler than he believed possible. Rips showed in her dress at the shoulder and she had the garment bunched tightly beneath her, as if it would keep him from her charms. He might have laughed at the pathetic sight if she hadn't started gettin' under his hide in a powerful way. Her incessant weeping made his nerves crawl.

His attention settled on the China girl and a knot formed in his belly. The priss annoyed him but that one . . . that one was as pleasant as sittin' on a spur and, greed be damned, he was close to shuttin' her yap permanent-like. Damn whore had been cussin' and spittin' at him since they hauled her yellow ass here. She wasn't afraid of him the way the others were. While that irked him it provided him with a much more serious problem: she likely wasn't trainable. And if she wasn't trainable she was worthless to him anyway. Chili-eaters liked them China gals for their intimate knowledge of how to please a fella and their ability to take orders. This one wasn't like to be any man's slave.

He stepped from behind the wheel. As he approached the railroad man's daughter, his boots thudded on the planks like gunshots and he watched her jolt with every step. Kneeling, his curved hook drifted to her face, stroking her cheek. She let out a strangled mew and tried to press herself into the rail. With a clipped laugh, he clacked her in the teeth and she let out a yelp. Blood dripped from her lip. He reckoned it would be swollen for a day or two but saw no permanent damage. He couldn't mess her up too bad with those men coming.

'I'm gonna enjoy tryin' you out, missy. You're gonna like it, too.' He grabbed her face with his good hand, jamming his fingers into her cheeks and pressing his lips to hers. He released the grip and she pulled away, tears streaming from her eyes and disgust on her face. He licked his lips, tasting the gunmetal flavor of her blood.

'Leave her alone, you sonofabitch!' The Asian woman spat at him, catching him on the cheek. Swiping the back of his hand across his face, he wiped saliva away, and scowled at the black-haired dove. That was another distressing turn of events: the China gal had befriended the railroad man's daughter. Who would have expected that from a whore?

'Snakes spit like that.' His voice came low, cold, but he saw no sense of fear or intimidation in her eyes, only defiance. 'Only thing a snake's good for is a new pair of boots.'

He straightened, drawing his sword and the blade flashed through the air, its tip coming to rest against the hollow of her throat. The railroad man's daughter gasped in fear but the Asian woman remained still, lip curling in spite.

'Do it, you bastard.' Her voice came steady, challenging. He might have respected that if it hadn't peeled his rattle so bad.

'You're a brave woman, China girl – and a stupid one. It would be better to accept what's gonna happen.'

'Or what? You'll kill me?' Her tone grew colder, threatening. 'You best do it right the first time, 'cause if you don't I'll cut your balls off.'

A burst of rage took him and he wanted to run the blade through her throat. He controlled the compulsion, barely, because he had a better way, one that would show the rest they couldn't talk that way to Morgan DeFete and get away with it.

He jerked the tip of the sword just enough to open a tiny wound. Blood trickled over her collar bone and down her chest. With a laugh, he withdrew the cutlass and slashed the bonds securing her to the rail.

She gazed up at him, rubbing the livid welts where the rope had bitten into her wrists.

'I can't train you, China gal. Get the hell outa here.'

'What?' For the first time he had heard something other than contempt in her voice and he almost smiled at her bewilderment.

'Get out, wench. You're no good to me: You'd make a piss-poor wife.'

Suspicion replaced the surprise in her eyes: She nodded to the other girls. 'What about them?'

'They stay. Surely a whore has no loyalty to others? You got choice: you can leave now or you can go with them and live in luxury with a man you don't know.'

'What those men got in mind ain't luxury...' She gazed at the other girls, lingering on the railroad man's daughter. He saw a hint of indicision in her eyes, then her lips mouthed a silent: 'I'm sorry.' Gaining her feet, she stood, wobbly at first, her sense of self-preservation overriding any compassion she might have felt for the rest.

She started towards the rope bridge leading to the ground. The men around the fire had stood and were looking up, a peculiar anxious expression tightening their faces.

Morgan laughed and swung the sword, bringing the flat of the blade to a stop an inch before her chest, blocking her exit down the bridge.

'You said I could go...' Her face went a shade paler for the first time since they'd brought her here.

'Not that way.' He ducked his chin towards the opening in the rail and the plank suspended over the water. 'Over there.'

The girl looked at the opening, deeper suspicion playing in her eyes but she moved over to the plank and peered down at the water below.

He grinned. 'You can swim, can't you, China gal?

Drop's only about ten feet and the water ain't that deep anyhow.'

Her gaze swung towards him, puzzlement in her eyes, as if she were trying to figure out what he was up to. 'There is a fence . . .' Her words came almost a whisper.

Was that fear he heard? He sure as hell hoped so. 'Can't make leavin' all that easy, can I? You'll get yourself some cuts most like, but it's worth freedom, ain't it, China gal?' He took a step towards her. Below the men backed up a few paces. He gazed at them, let out a shout. 'She makes it over that fence, boys, you let her go now, y'hear? Give her your horse, Higgins.' The hardcase nodded, but a nervous look lit his face and he seemed transfixed on the moat.

'Go on, China gal. 'Fore I change my mind.'

The other girls watched, spellbound by fear, and the Asian woman glanced back at them, then stepped on to the plank. Morgan came behind her and pressed the tip of the cutlass into her back, nearly causing her to fall.

She grew shaky as the plank wobbled, and held out her arms for balance.

A laugh whispered from his lips and she turned, looking at him with sudden fear and the realization that something was very wrong, though not sure just what. He swung the sword and she tried to run, intending to make a leap from the end of the plank and hurl herself over the moat and fence, he reckoned. The plank bowed and she lost her footing before reaching the end. She plunged straight down. She might have grabbed the plank and crawled back on to the deck if he hadn't stepped forward and jabbed her shoulder with the blade as she clutched for the board.

Arms windmilling, she struck the water with a great splash and everything seemed to go deathly still.

A heartbeat.

A great surge of water erupted from the moat, breaking

the silence. A monstrous dark shape exploded from the water as the Asian woman came above the surface and tried to swim for the fence. Huge jaws flashed, rows of razor-edged teeth gleaming in the early-morning sunlight. Men turned away, unable to watch as the girl's shrieks pierced the air.

Morgan laughed, peering over the rail at the fury of twisting limbs and flashes of black leathery flesh. The other girls started wailing, terror on their faces. The Chinese dove's shrieks were cut mercifully short when the enormous dark shape dragged her beneath the water. Crimson boiled up, blossoming over the surface.

Morgan turned to the terrified girls, gazing at them in turn. 'Anyone else want to leave?' The girls shook their heads, all except for the railroad man's daughter, who slumped against the rail, eyelids fluttering closed. He wished to hell she was made of more solid stuff and wouldn't keep passin' out every time he wanted to have a little fun with her.

Morgan looked back down at the bloody water. That had done it. Those gals would make right decent wives now. He smiled, right pleased with himself.

Marshal Trainor didn't move from his office chair the entire night. He knew he would have to ride out and inform Morgan about McCoy but, Christamighty, he wasn't too all-fired eager to do it. He hated going to that canyon. The thought of that god-awful creature the pirate kept in the moat turned his belly. Judas H. Priest, he didn't want to end up a meal for that loathsome thing. He'd damn well blow his own brains out before that monstrosity got ahold of him.

He shifted in the chair, back throbbing. Gazing out the front window, he watched the rising sun coat the street with honey-colored light. He couldn't put it off much longer; Morgan had to know McCoy was indeed a real threat; the manhunter knew far too much, though by all standards it was nothing specific. That didn't make much difference, in Trainor's estimation; McCoy was suspicious, knew the town's lawdog was involved in more than just protecting Lazarette's fine citizens and that was enough to make him a danger to their plans. Sooner or later something would lead to DeFete and jeopardize the whole operation. It would jeopardize Trainor's life if he didn't keep Morgan abreast of the situation.

He eased out of his chair, back grabbing and leg muscles cramping, making his stride wobbly. His heart thudded a beat faster. He reckoned that came more from the thought of encountering DeFete again than sitting in a position for too long. Plucking his hat from the wall peg, he jammed it on his head and went to the back door, inching it open. Peering outside, he made sure no one was watching, then scooted down the alley and across the street to the livery, where he boarded his horse. Fifteen minutes later he set out, keeping to the back street and angling around until he hit the trail leading out of Lazarette. He rode at a leisurely pace for a spell, giving the impression of a man out for a morning ride in case anyone had followed him. He even went so far as to meander offtrail at one point and spend fifteen minutes appearing to studying autumn foliage.

When he felt sure it was safe, he headed for the Galleon.

The sun glared high overhead by the time he reached the canyon and he shuddered despite the sweat trickling down his chest. Christamighty, sometimes he wished Morgan would up and fall into his own moat. That would put an end to things right nice, but then Trainor got a pretty price for them women and that wasn't something to just be tossed to the wind.

He guided the mount into the canyon, peering side to side. At first the area appeared deserted, then the sudden *shrik* of a Winchester lever made him sit straight up in the saddle. He swallowed and halted the horse. 'Hell, it's only me – Trainor!' His shout pierced the silence and for a moment all seemed deathly still.

Two men stepped from behind a high stand of brush, rifles leveled. They looked him over, then nodded.

'Go'wan,' one of them said, gesturing south with the rifle.

Trainor tipped a finger to the brim of his hat and gigged the horse into a walk, having no urge to reach the heart of the canyon any quicker than his nerves dictated. The platform coming into view, dread skewered him. At a glance, he saw three other gang members sitting around playing poker by a cold camp-fire. They paid him no mind far as he could tell but he knew his every move was being watched all the same. His gaze swept forward to the moat and his heart skipped. He recollected how many saloon gals had gone into that pool and damn near turned the horse around to head right on back to Lazarette.

Too late. Morgan appeared at the edge of the deck and scowled. Trainor drew up, dismounting, letting the reins trickle from his hands.

'What the hell you want?' Morgan's shouted challenge made him jolt, but he tried to conceal his fear.

He arched a hand over his brow against the stinging sunlight. 'I gotta talk to you about McCoy.'

'Permission granted to come aboard, Marshal.'

Christ, that kind of talk would sound right foolish if there weren't such a lethal edge to it, Trainor thought. He glanced at the water again, feeling his belly cinch. Did it appear vaguely red? Godamighty.

Gripping his composure, he went to the suspended bridge and started upward. Hands bleaching as he gripped the ropes, he was afraid if he peered over he might glimpse the huge shape gliding beneath the surface. What if those goddamn things jumped?

He made it topside without incident and blew out a sigh of relief. Morgan, peering at him, laughed. 'Hell, Marshal, my China gal had more balls than you.'

'Had?' Trainor looked over the four girls quivering against the rail, a plunging sensation in his gut. 'Where'd she go?'

Morgan grinned. 'Where the hell you think she went?'

'Jesus . . .' The marshal glanced back the way he came, knowing now why the water appeared red.

'What the hell's with McCoy?' Morgan asked, before Trainor could think on the girl's fate any longer.

'He came back yesterday after you left. Said he's gonna stay till he finds you.'

'You say something to make him suspect I'm here?'

Trainor didn't care for the look that crossed DeFete's face. He quickly shook his head. He had to be careful. He didn't know how much them damn things ate, but he figured one gal wasn't likely enough to fill its belly. With all that time he'd sat in his office he should have thought of a better story to feed Morgan.

'He's suspicious, is all. Said he would keep askin' if I'd seen the man on his poster till he got the answers he wanted.' Trainor didn't see a change in DeFete's demeanor so he added a lie. 'Says the fella on his dodger is you.'

Morgan's eyebrow arched. 'Did he, now?' The pirate leader went to the edge of the deck, leaning against the rail and gripping the top with his good hand. Tapping the wood with his hook, he remained silent and Trainor felt his legs go weaker, threatening to make him collapse.

Morgan swung around, voice snapping like a whip. 'You take Higgins and Trench back with you. Have them take care of McCoy and that gal with him. We can't afford no interference, not with them Mex buyers on their way.'

Trainor gave a stuttering nod, relieved he wouldn't be made into that creature's dinner.

'You are dismissed, Marshal.' Morgan went to the ship's wheel and gripped a protruding spoke. 'Don't waste much time gettin' gone. Feedin' time's comin' up again.'

Trainor winced and, forcing himself not to look down, took the rope bridge in three bounds. He rode back to town with the two men a hell of a lot faster than he had come . . .

Night swept over Lazarette with an ominous sense of portent. After waking with Coralie still in his arms, Trace McCoy had spent most of the day sullen and half afraid to look her in the eye. While neither spoke of the embrace, it created a brittle awkwardness between them. In some ways it left him more confused and empty, yet in others it made him feel almost alive and human for the first time in five years. He wouldn't have changed it but for the time being it was easier to pretend it hadn't happened. She had posed little objection when he insisted she stay behind in the room while he kept watch on the marshal. Her accession, after making him promise to inform her should there be a break in the case, wasn't the only surprise of the day.

Taking up a post near the lawdog's office, he had waited a good two hours, but Trainor had never come in. Suspicious, he had gone to the office only to find it empty. After questioning the livery attendant, he'd learned the lawman had set off on some early morning ride and hadn't returned. Disgusted at the fact his quarry had out-maneuvered him, Trace kept watch for his return most of the day but reckoned any chance he might have had at trailing him to Harrigan, if indeed that's where he had gone, had evaporated for the moment.

Returning to the hotel room, he discovered Coralie waiting on him, perched on the edge of the bed. A haunting sense of memory chilled him. Framed in dim lantern light, she looked so much like Karen it made him pause in the doorway, frozen in the past.

'Karen . . .' He wasn't sure if he had spoken or if the name had merely whispered in his mind.

'You get anything out of him?' Her voice came low and she looked hopeful.

Breaking the spell, he closed the door behind him and shook his head. 'Pains me to admit it, but the wiry little sonofabitch snuck out 'fore I got there this morning. Waited all day for him to come back but ain't likely it matters. He's done whatever he set out to do.'

She nodded, frowning. 'Reckon we should try the saloon for some dinner?'

He eyed her. 'Why the saloon? We can go to the café if you're hungry.'

'I want to try talkin' to the whores. I figure they'll be far more likely to talk to one of their own than a manhunter. Maybe they know somethin'.'

He shrugged. 'Reckon it's worth a try.' In fact, he doubted they'd find anything further but while he'd spent the day frustrated and disgusted with himself, he'd gotten plenty of time to think on the girl before him. He couldn't recollect a night of comfort spent since Karen's death, but last night, despite his nightmare, with her in his arms, was as close as he had come. He discovered he now had little desire to just drop her off in town and ride out after Harrigan alone, the way he had planned. Dinner in her company was suddenly a hell of a lot more appealing than eating jerky alone on some night-shrouded trail.

Moments later, they headed from the hotel, stepping on to the boardwalk. Chilly night air braced them and Coralie shivered. Hanging lanterns cast a cidery glow, marbling the shadows that shifted as the breeze swayed signs and lamps. His gaze centered on the lawdog's office; a light burned within now and he uttered a curse. The lawdog couldn't have returned more than a half-hour ago.

They started along the boardwalk, boots clomping a hollow rhythm. Coralie kept close to his side, maybe too close, but he made no move to push her away.

The street was deserted, but a sudden crawling sensation took him, a prickle of that sixth sense manhunters developed after years on the trail. It came as they passed before an alley, but it came too late.

The world seemed to fall on him and Coralie let out a high-pitched yell. A man grabbed him, swung him around. Something flashed towards his skull. He tried to jerk his head sideways but wasn't fast enough to avoid the blow completely. A gun butt glanced from his temple. Trace staggered, nearly going down.

Coralie shouted an unladylike curse and hurled herself at the first man. She flung her arms about his neck and clamped her legs around his hips, then did her best to scratch out his eyes.

The attacker gyrated, trying to throw her off, and let out a screech as she raked his face. 'Christamighty, Higgins, get her off'n me 'fore she tears my eyeballs out!'

'Shut the hell up, you idiot!' Higgins grabbed at Coralie, getting handfuls of her hair and yanking her backwards. He jerked her free and whirled her around, slamming her into a building wall. Rebounding, she crashed face first into the dirt. Dazed, she struggled to hands and knees.

The men converged on Trace, who was trying to shake the effects of the blow. His head reeled and streaks of ebony and amber whipped before his vision.

The man called Higgins circled, lunged. Trace looped a punch, but the blow, sloppy and desperate, missed.

Higgins angled left and grabbed him from behind, wrapping thick arms around Trace's chest and squeezing. The pressure forced the air from his lungs and he gasped for breath.

The second hardcase aimed a Smith & Wesson at Trace's chest.

'Wait till I ain't holdin' 'im, you sonofabitch!' Higgins's tone said he wasn't the least bit sure his partner wouldn't pull the trigger and kill them both.

'Just hold 'im still an' I'll shoot 'im in the thinkbox.' The second hardcase lifted the aim to Trace's head.

'Jesus H., are you plumb loco? You'll get me full of blood even if you don't bury me!'

'Stop yer goddamn complainin'. You know what Morgan'll do with us if we fail.' The hardcase stepped closer.

Trace recovered enough while the men were arguing to time his move for when the man with the gun came forward. He hoisted his feet, kicking out with all his might. The blow took the man square in the chest, hurling him backwards into a building wall. He managed to hold on to his gun, but stood shaking his head in an effort to clear his senses.

Feeling Higgins's grip slacken a fraction, Trace seized advantage of the hardcase's surprise. Anchoring his feet, he thrust backward, sending them both into the opposite wall. Higgins hit hard, his grip faltering.

Trace stamped a boot-heel on to the man's instep. The hardcase let out a wail of pain. Breaking free, McCoy whirled, throwing a roundhouse punch with little power. Higgins flung up an arm, partially blocking the punch, but the blow grazed the top of the head and sent him dancing backward.

Trace lunged, but the hardcase recovered and winged an uppercut that seemed to come from the ground. It snapped Trace's head up and slammed his teeth together. Stars exploded before his vision. He staggered. He wasn't sure what held him up but the hardcase wasn't about to give him a chance to retaliate.

Higgins stepped in, throwing a left hook. Pure instinct taking over, Trace ducked the blow and buried a snapping right in the man's belly. Air burst from the attacker's lungs and he doubled over.

Behind the manhunter, the second hardcase recuperated enough to get his gun leveled on the manhunter's back. Trace, staggering, heard the *skritch* of the hammer being drawn back and tried to turn, making it only half way before a shot rang out. He tensed, expecting to feel the bullet burn its way into his back.

It never happened. The gunman stuttered in his step, Smith & Wesson dropping from his nerveless fingers. Crumpling to the ground, the hardcase lay still. Behind Trace, Coralie stood clutching a smoking derringer with both hands. A look of stark fear showed on her face and she seemed frozen.

Trace got no chance to dwell on it because Higgins leaped, thrusting out with both arms to ramrod Trace backwards into the wall. Trace jabbed a knife-hand into the man's Adam's apple. Higgins squawked, gagged, and clutched at his throat. Trace brought an uppercut straight up the middle. The blow practically lifted the man off the ground, and Higgins collapsed like an old sack.

Panting, muscles quivering, McCoy went to Coralie, who hadn't budged. He forced her arms down and she started to tremble visibly.

'How long you had that on you?' He nodded to the derringer as she dropped it into her dress pocket.

'Years, but I ain't never had to use it. I think I'm gonna throw up . . .'

He took her in his arms, held her, and it seemed

suddenly so natural, as if he'd done it a hundred times before. 'It's all right, Coralie. You wouldn't have shot him he would have killed us both.'

'Who are those men? What'd they want with us?'

'I got a notion my little talk got the marshal antsy enough to go for reinforcements.'

'Reckon you won't be able to tell that to anyone, though, McCoy.'

The voice came from behind them and Trace turned to see Marshal Trainor standing on the boardwalk, a Colt aimed in their direction. 'Which one of you shot that man?'

Trace pushed Coralie behind him. 'I did. He attacked us with no cause. It was self-defense, Marshal, pure and simple.'

The marshal laughed. 'Reckon you won't be offended if I don't just take your word on that?' He came forward a few steps, a smug expression on his face.

'You know he's tellin' the truth, Marshal,' Coralie said. 'And he wasn't the one who shot—'

'Ma'am, I know no such thing.' The lawdog cut her off and Trace was just as glad. He would not let her take the blame for killing that man in his defense. A manhunter stood a much better chance in a courtroom than a whore, assuming the marshal let it go that far.

With the gun, the marshal gestured at the man sprawled in the dirt behind Trace. 'That other fella, McCoy, you kill him, too?'

'He's alive.' Trace saw only too clearly where things were headed and didn't like it.

The lawdog let out a thin laugh. 'Reckon when he comes to he'll likely tell the story a bit different. Likely he'll see it as murder. Bet he'll say you attacked him and his pal without provocation.'

Trace's belly cinched. The lawman had him and knew

it. 'Why you doin' this, Marshal?' He eyed the man intently, but Trainor didn't flinch.

'Why, because it's my duty, Mr McCoy. I knew you was trouble the moment you rode in. I tried to tell ya it'd be healthier to move on, but you wouldn't listen. You're under arrest, sir, for the crime of murder. Reckon you best not try anything and walk real slow-like towards the jail.'

'The hell he will!' Anger flashed across Coralie's face. 'I'll tell everyone who'll listen you're framin' him and I'll tell them I killed that man. Mr McCoy was just protectin' me.'

The marshal let out a derisive snort. 'Who'd believe a whore, missy? No one 'round these parts. I'm orderin' you to get out of town by dawn. You're still here when the sun rises I'll see to it you hang as an accessory.'

She started for him and Trace caught her arm, holding her back. 'Best do what he says, Coralie.' He turned her to face him. 'Won't help if he strings you up and he's right, no one's going to believe you. Looks like he put things together right well and I obliged by killing one of them.'

'I won't just leave you.' She suddenly kissed him but he pushed her away.

'Get the hell out of here! You're just a no-good whore anyway. I ain't got no use for you no more.' He said it as harshly as he could. He wouldn't let her risk her life for him. He saw pain burst into her eyes at his words and it tore him up inside, but it was for the best.

'You bastard . . .' Tears suddenly streamed down her face.

The marshal motioned with his gun. 'Christ, I hate to intrude on your little moment, but I got a cell waitin' to be warmed, McCoy. Now get a move on and keep your hands nice and high.'

Trace stepped away from Coralie, feeling her tearful

gaze drilling into his back as the marshal herded him towards the office. Once inside, the lawdog guided him to one of the three cells at the back.

'Put your arms through the bars and lace your fingers together. Then step back and spread your legs. I ain't takin' no chances with you.'

Trace complied, having little other choice and not caring to get back-shot.

The marshal reached around, unhitching Trace's gunbelt. It dropped to the floor and the lawdog kicked it out of the way. He slapped Trace's sides and boots, locating no further weapons, but stopping at a side pocket.

'What the hell's that?'

'Dominoes.'

The marshal nodded, obviously believing the bulge wasn't a weapon. The lawdog stepped back and motioned with the gun. 'Get in the cell.'

Trace withdrew his arms from between the bars and walked into the cell. A cot with a worn blanket flanked the back wall, beside it a rickety wooden table. Trace sat on the edge of the cot and watched the marshal lock the door then hang the keys on a nail at the opposite end of the room. The lawman holstered his gun then picked up Trace's rig and stowed it in a desk drawer.

'They payin' you a lot for this, Marshal?'

The lawdog lowered himself into his seat, smirking. 'Told you, I'm just doin' my job, McCoy. Reckon I got an airtight case once that fella comes to. Maybe we'll even hold ya for trial . . .' He laughed, plucking a cigar from the humidor and puffing it to life.

Trace kept his gaze locked on the man. 'What's he do with them gals he takes, Marshal?'

'Don't know what you're talkin' about.' The marshal drew a deep drag from the cigar, blowing smoke out in a slow stream.

'That pirate leader, Harrigan. He's the man pullin' your strings, ain't he?'

A flicker of something showed on the lawdog's face. Fear? 'Like I said, McCoy, I don't know what you're talkin' about. Now best you shut the hell up and let me enjoy my cigar, 'less you want me to think real hard on hangin' you in the mornin' and savin' the good folks of Lazarette the trouble of a trial.'

Trace sat back on the cot, and the marshal leaned back in his chair, jamming the cigar between his teeth and laughing to himself every so often as he encountered some thought he found particularly entertaining.

A hell of a predicament he had gotten himself into. He had wound up in brushes with lawmen in the past who cared little for the type of justice he doled out, but in every instance those men had been honest law-enforcers and the fellas he brought down wanted hardcases. In this case, he had a man likely in league with the enemy. The man Coralie killed might well have a stack of dodgers on him but in the end it would make no difference. The case would never go to trial. They would hang him way before that or put a bullet in his back under the excuse of a jail-break or some such.

Sighing, he leaned forward and pulled the pouch of dominoes from his pocket. As he dumped them on the table, the marshal glanced over, then went back to his cigar.

Trace started laying them out in a line, not really focused on the game but instead trying to figure a way out of the situation. Things looked damned dim in his estimation. He carried no other weapons and he reckoned he had hurt Coralie enough for her to ride out and let him rot. He prayed she'd give up on finding Harrigan before she got herself killed, and it struck him he was a hell of a hypocrite to be wishing something like that. But he found himself wanting more for her, wishing her some chance at the life he never had, at happiness.

He came from his thoughts, staring at the bones. Without realizing it he had somehow placed all the dominoes in descending order against each other until none remained.

He'd won. For the first time since he'd been playing. Here he was, trapped in a cell, a murderer awaiting his fate, and he'd finally won the blasted game.

'I'll be damned . . .' he muttered.

Hell, God had a more ironic sense of humor than Trace had given Him credit for . . .

Coralie watched the marshal take Trace McCoy to the office and disappear inside. She backed on to the boardwalk, glancing first at the dead man and the unconscious hardcase in the alley, shivering. She had never killed anyone and the thought of it made nausea twist in her belly. That fella deserved it, the way the gang leader deserved to die for what he had done, but the reality of seeing the man who lay dead by her hand sickened her, made her want to retch and reconsider going after Harrigan. She steeled herself, trying to drum it into her mind she had done the right thing because it saved Trace McCoy's life. Clutching her belly, she walked back towards the hotel before the second man awoke for another try at her.

She drew a deep breath of cool night air, her mind whirling and the memory of Trace's words biting at her heart. He had called her a whore, and it hurt, hurt like hell, though she had been called such a hundred times before. Not once had it caused the turmoil inside her it did now. He hadn't meant it; she felt sure of that, but it stung just the same. He wasn't the only actor in Lazarette tonight, she reckoned. She couldn't have called herself a very good judge of men if she hadn't seen through his attempt to get her out of harm's way. He proved his intent the moment he took the blame for shooting the hardcase. No one, especially a man, had ever stood up for her that way. But he was a piker when it came to deceit, and for that she was just as glad.

It hadn't been difficult to make herself cry and appear broken after he called her what he did. The tears might have even been real; she wasn't totally sure herself. But they had worked. She knew she had convinced him and the marshal she would leave town.

The act failed to solve the dilemma of getting him out of custody, however. That marshal would never let him get to trial; he would hang Trace before that happened and she doubted that moment would be long in coming. She needed to do something fast, while at the same time being careful to avoid getting hanged herself.

The notion occurred to her that risking her own life for another was a new feeling, though she had to admit she was as scared as she had ever been. It would have been so much easier to just ride on out of town, but something inside wouldn't allow that. Maybe it was part of what her pa instilled in her, but she couldn't deny it seemed to be strengthening the more time she spent around Trace McCoy. As if his character was somehow resurrecting her own, letting her see her soul the way it was meant to be.

Reaching the hotel, she glanced back to make sure the hardcase hadn't revived and followed her. The street appeared deserted, the only noise – laughter, shouts, curses – coming from the saloon.

The saloon . . .

An idea struck her, but it would take money and she had none to her name. But Trace did, in his saddlebags. It wouldn't be like it was stealing or anything, she reckoned.

She'd find a way to pay him back and didn't the end justify the means in this case?

A sinking notion stopped her. Just how would she pay him back? By whoring until she made the money? That would sure make him want to stay around her, wouldn't it?

She shook her head, feeling a clutch in her belly. She couldn't let herself think on that right now. She had to dwell in the moment, get him free first. The hows could come later.

She hurried into the hotel. When she reached the room, she grabbed his saddlebags and, rummaging inside, located the roll of greenbacks. Stuffing the money into her dress pocket, she rushed from the room.

As she stepped outside, her gaze swept the street for any sign of the hardcase or marshal. Seeing no one, she scooted towards the saloon. She pushed through the batwings and, eyes narrowing, scanned the room. The place looked like a hundred other such barrooms she had worked across the West. Durham smoke hung thick in the air and the stench of old booze, heavy perfume and puke assailed her nostrils.

Most of the bargals were heavyset and far from attractive. She selected the best-looking dove and threaded her way through the tables toward the gal, who stood next to the stairway leading to the upper level. Arm draped sensuously over the rail, breasts mounding from her bodice, she had a wooden smile saddled on her face and a dull but saucy look in her eyes. A laudanum addict, Coralie reckoned, and that made her task likely all the easier. Whores with drug habits weren't hard to buy.

Coralie approached the gal head on, trying to look more confident than she felt. Fact was, she was getting more frightened by the minute. Something inside had raised the stakes where Trace McCoy was concerned.

The woman eyed her. Young but hard, she had caked

on enough make-up to resemble a Kewpie doll. A purple sateen bodice hoisted her bosom; mahogany hair done in rings tumbled to her shoulders.

'You lookin' for work?' Coralie plucked the roll of greenbacks from her pocket.

The girl's face took on a peculiar turn, but she eyed the cash with a glint of greed. 'You one of them strange women?'

Coralie wagered her cheeks reddened for the first time in her life. 'Hell, no! I need your help and I'm willin' to pay for it. I've spent plenty of time workin' saloons myself.'

The girl cocked an eyebrow. 'Yeah, I reckon I can see that. What you want me to do?'

'Marshal's got a friend of mine over at the jail. I want to get him out.'

The girl gave her a skeptical expression. 'What's this friend s'posed to have done?'

'Marshal blames him for killin' a man, but that fella attacked us and he didn't shoot him anyway – I did.'

The girl laughed. 'That's a new one. Wouldn't swallow a word of it, neither, but for the fact that no-good marshal's got himself a habit of beatin' on his whores when he comes in. Don't reckon I really want to get on his bad side.'

'You wouldn't have to. Just pretend you got a thing for him and ring his bell. I'll give you a hundred dollars.'

'Christ on a crutch!' The girl's eyes lit up. 'That's enough for me to get right on out of this town, but the thought of bein' with that sonofabitch ain't real appealin'.'

Coralie slowly counted off bills, watching the girl's eyes follow every move. She felt vaguely guilty about manipulating the dove but what choice did she have? The marshal would hang Trace.

'I'll give you another fifty for your trouble. Take a bottle of whiskey and get him drunk till he passes out, then tell him his pecker was pleased as punch and he'll never know the difference.'

The girl appeared to think it over, but not for long. 'Reckon that much money's worth a beatin' anyway. Will fetch me enough medicine from the doc to kill the pain.' She snatched up the bills and stuffed them in her skirt.

NINE

The office door rattled open and Trace looked up to see a girl entering. Although young, her make-up was applied heavy enough to crack if she smiled too wide. Hair done in mahogany ringlets, it tumbled over smooth shoulders. Her bosom damn near hit her chin. A whiskey bottle in her left hand and a lustful expression on her too-red lips, she eased the door shut. The marshal eyed her, grinning like a cat who'd just discovered his tail.

'Well, hello there, honeypie.' Trainor jammed his cigar into the bottle-bottom ashtray and a lascivious gleam danced in his eyes. 'What can I do ya for?'

The girl flashed a coy smile and sashayed over to the desk. She dragged her fingertips along the edge and put on a display of shyness that would have befitted a schoolgirl. 'Well, Marshal, just that you usually come on into the saloon by this time of night. I sorta got to missin' ya.'

He nodded towards the cell. 'Got me a killer, missy.'

Her gaze flicked to Trace and she gave him a wink then looked back to Trainor. 'I been watchin' you with the other gals, Marshal. I had my eye on you for quite some time, now.' After setting down the whiskey bottle, she angled around to the back of the desk and eased on to the lawdog's lap. She leaned close, letting him get a good eyeful of her cleavage. 'Why don't you ever hire me, Marshal? I'm startin' to think you don't like me.'

He beamed, licking his lips and jutting out his chest like a prize bantam cock. 'Well, just savin' the best for last, I reckon.'

She giggled. 'Oh, Marshal, you sure know how to make a lady feel special. I bet if you asked real nice I'd give it to ya for free.' She leaned closer and flicked her tongue across his lips. He began to paw at her front, but she pushed him back and wagged a finger. 'Uh-uh, Marshal. I just wouldn't feel right doin' it in front of a killer. A gal's got her standards, you know.'

A foolish grin spread over his lips. 'Well, hell, I got me a room right upstairs. Nice feather bed just waitin' for some fluffin'.'

She slid off him, taking his hand and pulling him to his feet.

Trainor gave Trace a sarcastic smile. 'Don't go nowhere, y'hear?' He laughed and led the girl, who grabbed the whiskey bottle from the desktop, to the rickety stairway in the back. They went up and the room fell suddenly quiet.

Trace leaned back on the cot, alone but no better off than when the marshal was in the office. With his gunbelt in the drawer and the keys across the room, he had no chance of getting out of the cell. And no chance of tracking down Harrigan. Christ, what did it matter? He would be dead the moment Trainor got a rope around his neck. Harrigan would have the last laugh and Karen's spirit would wander forever restless.

A thud came from upstairs and he reckoned the marshal was going to be in a whole lot more arrogant mood by the time he got done dipping his wick.

A sound from across the room caught his attention; his gaze lifted to see the door opening. Coralie stepped inside, gazing about. She eased the door shut behind her.

'Would've been sooner 'cept I wanted to make sure the marshal had his tallywacker tied.' She smiled and in that moment he couldn't deny she was the brightest star in a black night.

'Thought I told you to get the hell out of Lazarette.' His tone belied the reprimand, coming with a lilt of excitement at seeing her. He stood, going to the bars.

An honest laugh escaped her lips. 'You best work on your actin' technique you expect to fool *me* any time soon.'

He nudged his head to the keyring hanging on the nail. Coralie headed for it, snatching up the keys just as a bootfall came from the back stairs, stopping her dead.

'You didn't really think I'd fall for that, did you, missy?' The marshal clomped down the stairs, gun drawn, muzzle centered on Coralie. Trace felt all hope drain out of him. Christ, he wished she had just ridden off the way he told her to.

'You must be fast on the trigger.' Her tone carried a blistering note of sarcasm.

He snorted. 'No, you might say that gal ain't particularly feelin' up to doin' me no favors right now, but I reckon she'll come around later – throw the keys on the desk, ma'am.'

A flash of anger in Coralie's eyes told Trace she was debating hurling herself at the marshal, trying to wrestle the gun away from him. She didn't have a chance and Trace said a silent prayer she would let go of the foolish notion. A defeated look washed over her face. She tossed the keys on to the desk, glaring at Trainor the entire time.

'Let her go, Marshal.' Trace's fingers tightened on the bars, going white. 'She ain't done nothin' to you.'

He glanced at Trace. 'And have her come back for another try at breakin' you out? I only let her go 'cause I didn't think a whore would give a damn. I reckoned she would save her own ass, but obviously she's got somethin' for you. She's too much trouble. I ain't about to let her just walk away again.' He turned to Coralie and gave her the once over. 'You ain't so bad lookin' but I reckon you ain't pretty enough to take to the Galleon. You got yourself a crooked nose and too many lines. Doubt you'd fetch a high price.'

'So what do you do with me, Marshal? Throw me in jail and blame me for murder, too?'

'Hell, no! I told you I caught you in town what I'd do. Gonna have me a hangin'. Reckon since you broke in here and tried to kill me you gave me no choice. Course, you killed that other gal, too, least you will have by the time I get done with her.'

'Christ, no!' Trace yelled, anger making his muscles tremble. 'Hang me if you want, but don't hurt her.'

The marshal glanced at Trace and a vicious smile played on his face. 'Men like you always got control over every situation and everyone, don't they, McCoy? You're kinda like Morgan. You decide life or death and it makes you just wanna dance, I reckon. It feels goddamn good to have that choice, don't it? I got the power now, McCoy, and I damn well like it.'

Muscles balled to either side of Trace's jaw. 'I'll kill you, Marshal. I swear I will.'

'Now that's right funny, Mr Manhunter, seein' as how you ain't exactly in the position to be makin' threats.'

Trainor looked back to Coralie, who had gone a shade whiter. He motioned with the gun for her to head to the door.

'Noooo!' Trace screamed as they went out. 'You sonofabitch, nooo!' The door closed and he pressed his forehead against the bars, fury singing through his veins and despair overwhelming his being. The lawdog would hang Coralie and nothing he could do would stop it. It was his fault for letting her ride along with him, his fault for placing her life in danger, and now he couldn't save Coralie, the way he couldn't save Karen.

Help me . . .

'Christ, nooo . . .' he whispered, everything inside him screaming. Flashes of that day at the stream melded with the image of Coralie hanging from a rope.

A noise from the back broke his thoughts and his gaze jerked to the stairs. The bargirl took a tentative step downward, clutching to the rail for support. Face a palate of black, blue and red, her lips were swollen, bleeding, and livid welts nested beneath both eyes. Tears had tracked kohl streaks down her cheeks; smudged coral and smeared lipstick made her look pervertedly clownish. Skirt and bodice torn in places, she tried another step down and stumbled, nearly falling the rest of the way. Only her grip on the rail prevented her from breaking her neck.

Trace noticed rope burns on her wrists and knew the lawdog had tied her but somehow she had gotten loose.

She reached the bottom and gazed at him, glassy-eyed. 'He . . . hurt me . . .' Her words came slurred, mumbled, as if speaking took great effort.

The sight sickened Trace, infuriated him even further. 'You have to let me out of here. He's gonna kill Coralie.'

The dazed expression deepened. 'Cor . . . alie?'

'The woman who hired you.'

Her face darkened and he realized instantly he'd made a mistake. 'It's her fault this happened to me!'

Trace shook his head. 'No, it ain't her fault. She's innocent, way you are. Blame it on that lawdog, miss. He's the one who hurt you. Let me out of here and I'll see he pays for it. He'll hang Coralie if you don't, then come back and kill you.'

She stared at him, as if struggling to form words. 'You'll kill him for me?'

He nodded. 'I got a bullet with his name on it.'

She nodded and pushed herself away from the steps. Staggering towards the desk, she almost went down, and for a breath-holding moment he thought she would collapse. She reached the desk, falling against it heavily, then grasped the keys and tried to turn. The willpower seemed to desert her then. With a strangled mew she fell to the floor, arm outflung. The keys skidded across the boards but stopped too far from the bars for him to reach. The girl went still, her breathing raspy, labored.

Mind racing, he went to the table. Throwing it over, he jammed a boot against the base while grasping a leg. He gave a sharp jerk and the leg snapped free.

He returned to the cell door, he lay on the floor and stretched an arm through the bars, holding the table leg out before him. The leg didn't quite reach, only an inch or less separating it from the keys, but it might as well have been a hundred feet.

Sweat broke out on his forehead and he strained to extend the leg, feeling his arm damn near come out of its socket. An eternity seemed to trickle by until he felt the tip of the leg touch the keyring. Applying pressure, he sought to drag the ring towards him; the keys came forward only fractions before the leg slipped. He let out a curse. Heart pounding against his ribs, he made another try at the ring, this time getting it easier. Arm starting to quiver, palm slick with sweat, he inched the keys towards him.

A final pull brought the ring close enough for him to get his fingers around the brass rim. Blowing out a sigh of relief, he leaped to his feet and jammed a key into the lock. He threw open the door, ran to the desk and yanked open the drawer, pulling out his gunbelt. After strapping it to his waist, he paused to inspect the bargirl. She was alive but he doubted she would remain so if he didn't get her medical attention. He had no time for that now.

Coralie might already be dead. With a stab of regret, he ran for the door, flinging it open and stepping out into the night.

He recollected noticing the gallows as he and Coralie rode into the town and he ran along the boardwalk in that direction. His heart pounded against his ribs and his breath beat out in staggered gasps. Christ, if he was too late he'd blow the lawdog's brains clear to hell.

The gallows rose up in the moonlight about a hundred yards down and his belly plunged at the sight. He spotted two figures poised on the platform. The marshal gestured with his gun, forcing Coralie to slip the noose over her head. A bolt of relief washed through him at seeing her alive, but in another moment that situation would change.

'Marshal!' Trace's shout snapped the lawdog's head around. The manhunter's hand swept towards his gun.

A startled look struck Trainor's face and he swung his Colt towards Trace, at the same time yanking the lever to his right. The trap door beneath Coralie's feet released with a shudder.

'Noooo!' Trace yelled, heart dropping even as his gun came level on the marshal.

Coralie plunged downward, at the last instant grabbing the rope above her head and struggling to hang on. Trace thanked the Almighty Trainor hadn't gotten time to bind her wrists, because the move prevented her neck from snapping. She kicked out, suspended in mid-air, fighting to keep from suffocating.

Events seemed to occur in exaggerated motion. The clomping of his boots hitting the planks roared like thunder in his ears. Trainor's shouted curse reverberated through the night and the bore of his gun centered on the manhunter's chest.

Instinct taking over, Trace's finger twitched against his

Colt's trigger. He had no time to concentrate on aim or adjust for his forward motion.

The shot echoed through the brittle air in slow crashing waves. Through senses made hyperaware by fear for the young woman's life, he swore he could see the bullet burst from the Peacemaker's barrel in a flash of flame and blue smoke.

The bullet missed, sailing off into the night.

Trainor, fright on his face, jerked the trigger in reflex, but his own aim was hasty, his hand quaking. Lead plowed into the boards a foot to Trace's left.

The manhunter squeezed off another shot. Crimson exploded across the marshal's chest as the bullet punched through bone. The impact kicked Trainor backwards off the platform and he slammed down flat on his back in the dirt, gasping.

Trace shoved the Peacemaker into its holster as he reached the platform. With a leap he was upon it. Locking his arms about Coralie's waist, he hoisted her up enough to take the pressure off her neck. She pried at the noose, getting it loose enough to slip over her head. He lowered her to the platform and held her. She sobbed into his chest.

'Christ, McCoy, what took you so long?' she said through tears, half choking.

He let out a relieved breath. 'We have to help that gal you sent. She's in a bad way.' She nodded as he broke the embrace and looked into her tearful eyes. He had come too close to losing her and the feeling made his legs tremble.

He went to the edge of the platform and jumped down, Coralie following suit. Kneeling beside the marshal, he looked the man over. He glanced up at the young woman, who had wrapped her arms about herself and was shaking visibly. 'He's alive but I reckon he won't live out the night.

Lot of blood soaking into the dirt.'

'He ain't gonna be missed.' Her voice came cold, laced with anger.

'We best get him to the doc, too. I reckon he knows where that gang's hid out and if we got a chance to make him talk . . .'

A half-hour later they had the saloon girl and dying marshal in a bed in the sawbones' back room. The older man had bandaged up the dove and she lay unconscious with enough laudanum in her system to keep her out for the remainder of the night. She would live, though painfully for a spell. Trainor had broken a number of ribs, and she would go through life missing a handful of teeth.

The marshal was a different story. Pure orneriness kept him hanging on to life, but he wouldn't survive much longer. He'd lost too much blood and Trace's bullet had punctured a lung.

Trace stood over him, praying he would regain consciousness long enough to be forced into telling where the gang was holed up.

Trainor's eyes flicked open, reflecting a glassy look of terror. 'Am I . . . am I gonna make it?' The man's voice came liquidly, weak. His gaze focused on Trace and for an instant some spark of human compassion made him feel almost sorry for the sonofabitch.

The feeling died almost instantly, replaced by anger when he thought of what the man tried to do to Coralie. Trace grabbed the man's collar. 'I told you you owed my friend an apology . . .' He said it through gritted teeth and twisted the man's shirt, causing him a gasp of pain. The doctor stood by, on the verge of reproach, but Trace flashed him a look that stifled any interference.

The marshal's watery gaze flicked to the young woman. 'Go to hell . . . McCoy . . .'

Fury overwhelming him, he hoisted Trainor up by the

collar and slammed him back into the bed. The marshal let out a strangled bleat of pain. 'Ain't askin' you again, Marshal. You want to live out the night you best say it.'

'Trace, it ain't important . . .' Coralie whispered behind him.

But it was important, for no reason he could have articulated. Some sense of justice and chivalry, perhaps even some deeper emotion he was little prepared to admit, demanded it. 'Say it or I'll kill you right now, Trainor . . .'

'See here, Mr McCoy!' The doc took a step forward. 'The man's dyin'!'

Trace didn't turn around. 'We're all dyin', Doc. Just a matter of when.' He drew his Peacemaker and placed it against Trainor's temple. 'How soon you want to go, Marshal?'

Trainor coughed, blood bubbling from the corner of his mouth. He started to tremble, looked at Trace then at Coralie. 'I'm . . . sorry . . .' The whisper was nearly inaudible.

'Tell me where that gang is, Trainor.' Trace thumbed back the hammer.

It was too late. The lawdog's eyes fluttered shut and a shuddery breath died on his lips. McCoy wasn't the least bit sorry to see the sonofabitch go.

He stood, holstering his piece, then looked at Coralie, who had wrapped her arms tight about herself. He saw the rope burns about her neck and any guilt he might have felt over hastening the marshal's death vanished.

'You're a cold man, Mr McCoy.' The doc shook his head and went to the body.

'Am I?' Trace's expression remained stony. 'That man tried to kill both these women and likely is involved with a gang that murders and kidnaps innocent daughters and bar doves alike. Don't reckon he deserved much sympathy.'

The doc nodded a somber nod and pulled the sheet over the body.

'Well that's that.' Coralie's voice sounded drained of hope.

He nodded, sighing. 'We'll find that man, Coralie. He's gonna come lookin' for the marshal sooner or later and then—'

'And then what?' Her voice rose, laced with emotion. 'We can just shoot him and go on with our lives?' She turned away and he felt suddenly awkward. He wasn't sure what he had expected her to say but that wasn't it.

'Thought you wanted that man dead for what he done to you.'

She turned back to him, tears shimmering in her eyes. 'Yes – no – I don't know what I want, now. I want Chinadoll back and I want that man to pay, but I don't know if I want this to be over, McCoy. I just don't know.'

Trace reckoned he knew all too well what she meant, but could he tell her he felt the same? Would it mean betraying Karen's memory, having feelings for . . .

A whore.

Easier to sidestep it, at least for the moment, he shook his head. 'Choice ain't ours any more. That man's gonna come here and when he finds his man dead he's gonna go after who killed him. I'll be waitin' on him when he does.'

'And what about me, McCoy? Hell, I want him dead for what he done more than you know and I want my friend back alive. I'll see this through 'cause I got no choice, but I want to know if there's somethin' beyond it.'

He looked at the floor, back to her. 'We'll find your friend and we'll find Chadburn's daughter. Marshal said something about not takin' you to the galleon; reckon that means they kept them girls alive.'

'We got no notion where or what this galleon is. Those

girls might be dead by the time that bastard comes lookin' for us.'

'Galleon Canyon?'

Trace turned to see the doc looking at them, eyebrow raised. 'What did you say?'

' 'Bout a half-day's ride south of here, place called Galleon Canyon, on account of it looks kinda like a big boat. Nothing much there, but might that be the place you folks are lookin' for?'

A measure of hope rose within him. 'Doc, I reckon you just might have saved me a hell of a lot of trouble.'

The older man shrugged. 'Or given you more if this fella you been talkin' about is as bad as you say.'

As Higgins rode hell-bent into the canyon, Morgan DeFete watched him from the platform deck. The hardcase came in alone and Morgan reckoned that was a piss-poor sign. Something had gone wrong. Again. Frowning, he threw a glance at the four women behind him and each shuddered as his gaze fell upon them. A clipped laugh escaped his lips, but it held no hint of humor. He didn't cotton to things going wrong. In fact, it made him downright peeled and one of those women was going to pay for that, most likely that railroad man's daughter. 'Bout time she became a woman anyway.

Higgins drew up and jumped from the saddle. Stopping at the base of the rope bridge, he glanced at the moat. The wavering light from torches set up along the base of the platform cast eerie light over the black water. The hardcase then swung his gaze upwards to Morgan. 'Permission to come aboard, sir?'

'Aye, mate.' Morgan's one-eyed gaze didn't waver from the hardcase as he bounded up the bridge.

'Trench is dead!' Higgins blurted. 'So's the marshal.'

'How?' Spittle flew from Morgan's lips. His left arm

swung up, hooking Higgins's shirt, half lifting him off the deck.

Higgins ran a tongue over his lips, face pinched with fear. 'That McCoy fella, we tried to kill him and that gal way you wanted, but she had a gun. She killed Trench and McCoy knocked me out. When I came to I saw the marshal leadin' her to the gallows but that manhunter came chargin' out of Trainor's office and shot him.'

A knot of anger twisted in Morgan's belly. Christ, it was worse than he thought. 'You sure he's dead? Don't need that coward runnin' his mouth off about this place.'

'Looked like he was hit pretty bad. I reckon he breathed his last 'fore he hit the ground, but I didn't stay to find out.'

Fury overwhelming him, Morgan hurled the man backward. Higgins stumbled, hitting the rail and grasping it with frantic fingers to keep himself from going over the edge.

DeFete didn't care a lick for the way things were lining up. Two more of his men dead, one his gal-broker. Add that to Crawford, who'd never returned, and it made for a powerful run of bad luck. He cast another glance over the women tied along the rail. Hell, a lot of money came from pirating flesh, more than all his raids put together. Without Trainor he would need a new middleman but that would take time. Hanging on to those girls much longer might prove a risk. Maybe he should just throw them all in the moat and be done with it.

No, risk or not, too much money was involved and those chill-eaters were already on their way. He could have Higgins meet them, bring them here for the payoff.

That meant he had to do something about McCoy and that bargal immediately.

McCoy. Was he just a manhunter on a case? Or something more? Morgan struggled to recollect, focusing on the marshal's description of the man again. Why was he familiar? A vague recollection struggled to form, a day long ago when he was still John Harrigan. A stream? Yes, that was it. Beside a stream, his gang had come upon young lovers, a sight that disgusted Morgan no end. They'd decided to have a little fun, taking the woman and killing the man.

Killing the man. No, that couldn't be McCoy, because they'd left that fella for dead. Hadn't they? Could that man have somehow lived? Christ, they'd beaten the hell out of him so bad Morgan didn't see how it was possible.

What about the girl? He felt reasonably certain she was the gal he'd taken at the saloon in Danton, a friend of that China gal's, but who'd have thought a whore would come lookin' for revenge? Christ, it just wasn't natural.

Morgan's gaze focused on Higgins, who poised against the rail with a frightened look on his face.

'You and Harper head back to town at dawn. Take care of that manhunter and whore this time. Bring me one of his ears. You fail again and you'll be goin' for a swim . . .'

Higgins gave a jerky nod and scurried down the bridge. Morgan went to the ship's wheel and gazed out into the torch-lit night, losing himself in the dark oceans of his mind.

TEN

As false dawn painted the sky in ash, Trace McCoy strapped on his gunbelt and gave Coralie Duvalier one last look. Although he'd promised to wake her and going back on his word sent a stab of guilt through his belly, he reckoned it was best to let her sleep. He'd reached the decision with a mixture of selfishness and concern. He had waited too long to put a bullet into John Harrigan and refused to let even her rob him of that satisfaction. The bastard would die for what he'd done to Karen, to the life Trace McCoy had been denied. As well, he would see to it the outlaw caused Coralie no more pain than he had already, nor would he allow her to risk her life aiding him again. The risk of failure was too great and Harrigan would do far worse to her than Trainor.

In the dim light she looked more like a heavenly angel than a fallen one. He leaned down and kissed her cheek, wondering whether he would live to see her again. The outlaw might well kill him and not so long ago that wouldn't have mattered so much. Now, somehow it did. He found he wanted to come back to her. The notion struck him he could have loved her, perhaps did, despite what she was. On the trail, she asked him what lay beyond John Harrigan and even now he couldn't answer that, but if indeed the Lord granted him a life he prayed it included her.

The moment the door closed Coralie's eyes snapped open and she propped herself up on an elbow. Her fingers went to the place on her cheek where he had kissed her. A shivery warmth spread through her innards she'd rightly never experienced.

She loved him.

How it was possible for a woman like her to care about a man, she didn't know, but it brought a fragile smile to her lips. She had longed for this moment for so many years and hidden dreams, doubting she would even recognize it if it came.

But she did recognize it, and it unearthed a rush of protective feelings that was nearly overwhelming. She wasn't about to let him go after that outlaw alone. While she had decided she would let him have the satisfaction of killing Harrigan, she refused to lose Trace McCoy and the chance at something that would likely never come her way again. Just getting Chinadoll back alive and knowing the outlaw had paid for the way he violated her was enough.

She had caught his lie last night when he told her he would wake her, but through the lie she had seen concern in his eyes . . . and maybe more. The notion he had done it to protect her made her forgive him without question, because it told her he cared and cared deeply. He somehow looked beyond what she was; maybe he didn't accept it, but perhaps he understood in some small way.

She swung her legs out of bed and pulled on her dress, then checked to make sure she'd reloaded the derringer. Hurrying to the door, she slipped out into the hallway and made her way from the hotel. The doc had told them the canyon's location but her nag of a horse wasn't like to make any time gettin' there. Still, she had to mix haste with her caution or Trace would gain too big a lead on her. That might mean the difference between life and death.

A sense of destiny washed over Trace McCoy as he rode the trail towards the Galleon Canyon. Years of searching, suffering and seething fury were coming to an end. Five years of revenge-driven hell. While Harrigan's death would not alleviate the grief, the loss, the constant longing for a life that never was, it sure as hell would bring Karen some measure of justice.

He gripped the reins tighter, hands bleaching, nails digging into his palms.

The forest rose to either side of the trail and shadows swayed across the hardpack. Sunlight filtered through evergreen boughs and glistened from dew-coated leaves. Low hills studded with cottonwood, fir and aspen, and strewn with boulders rose to his right. The terrain left plenty of places to conceal a bushwhacker but Harrigan couldn't know Trace was coming. Could he?

One hardcase was left alive . . .

He drew a deep breath. Yes, only one of the men who'd attacked him and Coralie last night had met death. In the flurry of events occurring after his arrest, Trace had forgotten a second man remained free to ride back, and inform the pirate leader of their failure. Would Harrigan make a move? Trace shot a glance along the trailsides, searching for any sign of threat, but everything appeared tranquil, only the morning birds singing. He shook off a prickle of apprehension.

A mile whisked past as Trace drove his horse into a faster gait. Anxiousness made him push the animal to its limit, and with each passing mile he felt that destiny swelling, sending images of the past careening through his mind and hate singing through his veins.

'Harrigan . . .' He muttered the name through clenched teeth. 'I'm coming for you, you sonofabitch.'

A commotion on the trail ahead tore him from his thoughts. Lost in bitter reverie, he hadn't noticed two men thundering towards him until they were barely twenty yards away. His belly dropped, the realization these men belonged to Harrigan's gang instant and blood-chilling.

He reined up but the time for evasive maneuvering had passed. The men bore down on him, splitting off, skidding to a stop at either side of his mount.

His expression became stony, eyes slightly narrowed, brow cinched. His gaze swept across their faces, but he recognized only one, Higgins, the man who attacked him in the alley the previous night.

'Well, well, McCoy . . .' A vicious light danced in Higgins's eyes. His face was lumpy, a map of livid bruises from the beating administered by Trace. 'You just saved us a passel of trouble comin' for you.'

Trace's gaze centered on the man and his right hand slackened on the reins, ready to go for his gun. Weighing the odds, he reckoned he might take out one but doubted he could swing around and get the second before the hardcase put lead in his chest.

'Best get out of my way, Higgins, or die where you're sittin'.' Trace kept his tone cold, even.

Higgins let out a harsh laugh. 'You got lucky last night, manhunter; that ain't gonna happen twice.'

Trace glanced at the hardcase to his right, back to Higgins. 'You weren't with Harrigan five years ago. I got no beef with you. Get out of my way and you walk away livin'.'

For a heartbeat the hardcase appeared to think it over. 'Don't know what the hell you're talkin' about or who this Harrigan is, but my boss wants you dead and I ain't about to risk what might happen if I don't get the job done right this time—'

Trace saw no other choice and made the decision instantly. Instinct taking over, he twisted left before Higgins had even stopped speaking. Foot sweeping out of the right stirrup as he grabbed for the man beside him, he came half out of his saddle. He clutched a handful of the man's shirt, yanking.

The hardcase, taken by surprise, lost hold of his reins. Trace twisted and threw himself sideways. Both men parted from the saddle and slammed into the hardpack. The impact jarred the breath from the hardcase's lungs and Trace came down atop him. McCoy tried to roll off and gain his feet so he could bring his gun into play, but the man recovered faster than he expected.

Higgins grabbed handfuls of Trace's shirt, hauling him down. They rolled in the dirt, the hardcase trying to slam an elbow into Trace's face, jab a finger into his eye, even biting at him to gain the advantage.

Trace tried to stab a knife-hand into his throat but the bandit was ready for the move and jerked his knee towards Trace's groin. McCoy twisted, taking the impact on the thigh. He snapped a short punch into the man's face. The blow came with little power but Higgins's bruises were obviously paining and the impact had more effect than it would have had under ordinary conditions.

Seizing the slight advantage, Trace tried to yank free of the man's grip and gain his feet.

He didn't make it. Half-way up, a blinding flash exploded before his eyes as a boot-heel collided with the back of his skull. The second hardcase had wasted no time climbing from his horse and aiding his partner.

Staggering, senses spinning, Trace struggled to reach his feet under pure force of will. The trail whirled before him and a second stunning pain ripped across his jaw, as

Higgins jumped up and fired an uppercut.

Trace's legs turned rubbery and he went over flat on his back, the hardcase's laugh echoing in his ears.

Hands grabbed bunches of his shirt and hauled him to his feet.

'Hold 'im, Harper!' Higgins shouted and the second hardcase clamped both arms about Trace's chest.

McCoy's vision started to clear and he saw Higgins's leering face before him. The 'case was dragging a forearm across his mouth, swiping blood from his lips.

'I'm gonna enjoy this, McCoy. Then I'm gonna blow your brains out and cut off an ear for DeFete.'

Higgins pistoned a blow into Trace's belly that forced all the air from his lungs in an explosive *woof*. A second blow damn near shattered his jaw.

Swirls of blackness threatened to eclipse his mind and suddenly the images from his nightmares crowded his vision. Five years ago, Harrigan and his men, beating him by the stream. The blows coming in slow motion, each inflicting incredible pain, each impact ringing like Winchester shots. Her screams ululating through time and space until everything inside him just went berserk.

Help me . . .

A yell burst from his lips and for an instant Higgins, fist poised in mid-air, peered at him as if he had just stepped on a scorpion.

Trace refused to let it happen again, not this close to finding Harrigan. If he died here he would have no way of stopping the hardcases from heading to town and murdering Coralie. Karen's death would never be avenged. It was no game of dominoes; it was everything that made up a man, even an empty one.

Taking advantage of Higgins's surprise, Trace hoisted his legs, snapping both boot-heels into the hardcase's groin. Higgins let out a sharp gasp and doubled, then collapsed, screaming 'Bastard!' over and over until vomit streamed from his mouth and splattered the trail.

The hardcase holding Trace was caught only slightly less by surprise. McCoy twisted, driven by the dark thing of vengeance inside him. Harper struggled to regain control, hold on, but Trace planted his feet and pivoted. Using the man's weight against him, he hurled the hardcase over his left shoulder. The man slammed into the dirt, cursing.

Trace, panting, started for Harper before he got a chance to recover, but the man wasn't hurt, merely surprised. He leaped up, hand slapping for his Smith & Wesson.

McCoy's hand swept for his own gun. Practiced over five years, the maneuver came smooth and without thought. In fluid motion the Peacemaker slid from its greased holster and streaked upward, centering on the rising hardcase, whose own hand was nowhere near as fast or skillful.

Harper barely managed to get out his gun before Trace feathered the trigger. A blast shattered the silence and the bandit staggered backwards, gun flying from his grip. A crimson starburst erupted on his chest; he went down on his back, gasping, blood bubbling from his lips.

Trace wasted no time surveying his work. Higgins, vomit stringing from his lips, was staggering to his feet, one hand clutching to his crotch, the other fumbling to get his six-shooter free of its holster.

McCoy pivoted, swinging the Colt's aim and triggering another shot. Higgins skipped backwards, smashing into the hardpack, limbs twitching in a death dance.

Trace holstered his Peacemaker and leaned over, hands on his knees. His breath beat out in hot gasps and his entire body shook.

At last his head lifted, and his gaze went from one hard-case to the other. Both were dead and he felt no remorse or guilt. They deserved what they got as far as he was concerned.

He went to the men's horses and sent them galloping in the direction of town. No need to have them find their way back to the canyon to warn Harrigan something was amiss.

He mounted and gigged his own horse south, body aching, blood running from the corner of his mouth.

The sun jumped a handspan across the sky and when Trace approached the entrance to Galleon Canyon he slowed. The opening gaped at him like the gate to Hell. Scraggly branches jutted from its sides and scrub pine and brush grew unbridled. Plenty of places to conceal a look-out. His eyes narrowed, searching for any signs of danger. He angled the horse right, where the trail swept upwards and hugged the outer parameters of the canyon.

A hundred feet on, he reined up and dismounted, tethering the bay to a piñon branch. Half-crouched, he scooted towards the opening. Drawing his gun, he kept close to the right side of the entrance.

A measure of surprise gripped him at encountering no guards, but reckoned Harrigan might be low on men after losing four over the past few days.

As he made his way deeper into the canyon, his heart pounded with anticipation. Before him, a hundred yards on, rose a platform surrounded by a makeshift moat. His breath caught. The platform vaguely resembled a ship and a figure in a duster and battered Stetson stood on its deck, gripping a polished wooden steering wheel. The spectacle would have been insane, laughable, had lives not been at stake – lives and justice. Trace had no idea what events transformed John Harrigan into this Western-day pirate and he rightly didn't care. A loco hardcase bled as easily as a sane one.

He edged closer. Blood rushed in his veins and his face heated with fury.

Harrigan!

Different with the patch and hook, though he noted the same arrogant posture and blocky build. John Harrigan had not vanished into Western legend; the man was alive and continuing his reign of terror in the guise of some lunatic buccaneer.

Every bitter emotion Trace had suffered in the past five years raged inside him now. Anxiousness made him want to draw his gun and shoot the man where he stood, but the distance was too great. He couldn't risk it and the self-ish hate inside brought a need to be looking into Harrigan's eyes when the bullet plowed into the outlaw's black heart.

Trace angled right, moving with caution so he would not attract the attention of a man he spotted sitting on a deadfall near a burnt-out camp-fire, whittling away at a piece of branch. One man. Was that the remainder of Harrigan's gang?

Face pinched as he crept forward, attention focused on the man sitting on the log. If he were going to get to Harrigan, he needed that hardcase out of the way but he saw no method of accomplishing that without a commotion.

Peacemaker clearing leather, he leveled on the bandit. A twig snapped beneath Trace's boot and the fellow's head jerked up, a shocked expression hitting his face. He dropped his branch and knife.

Trace gestured with the gun. 'Get up.'

Trace froze, a chill slithering down his spine. A sound had come from behind him and he swiveled his head to see a man stepping from behind a boulder.

A harsh laugh sounded from the deck of the platform. McCoy looked up to see Harrigan gripping the rail with his good hand, staring down at him.

'You didn't think I'd completely trust my men to kill

you, did you? They messed it up once, McCoy. Reckon I didn't figure they'd do the job any better this time. I expect you saw to their punishment?'

That voice. Harsh, grating, inhuman. The voice that had echoed through a thousand nightmares.

At the sound of it rage overwhelmed Trace McCoy. He refused to fail, not when he had gotten this close.

He whirled, swinging the Peacemaker around to the second hardcase. A startled expression slapped the man's face. He clearly hadn't expected the move but damn near blew off Trace's head all the same.

A thundering blast came from the hardcase's Smith & Wesson. Trace's hat flew from his head, the bullet missing him by only an inch.

Trace squeezed the trigger in reflex. The hardcase skipped backward, gun flying from his grip.

The man went down, unmoving.

Trace spun, just as the first bandit went for his own gun. He blasted a shot and the hardcase jolted, stumbling over the log and hitting the ground before his piece cleared leather. He lay gasping, crimson flowering across his chest.

Trace drew a sharp breath and tried to swing his gun upward, fire a hasty shot at Harrigan, but he was too late. A blast filled the canyon with thunder and the gun leaped out of Trace's hand. Blood streamed down his arm from the hole where lead had punched into his biceps.

A laugh followed, mocking him, nearly as thunderous as the shot and infinitely more damning.

Harrigan held a smoking Smith & Wesson and peered down with contempt. 'Permission granted to come aboard, McCoy – 'less you want me to shoot you where you stand.'

With a disgusted sigh, Trace walked toward the rope bridge. Pain skewered the length of his arm and his heart pounded against his ribs. He glanced at the moat, brow knotting as he caught a glimpse of something large and undefined moving beneath the water. Paying it little mind, he made his way up the bridge.

On deck, he noted four women tied up along the rail. Three were unfamiliar but he recognized the fourth from her likeness: Chadburn's daughter. His gaze swept across the terrified faces, finding none was Asian, and a sinking feeling hit his belly.

Attention shifting to Harrigan, he saw the man had a peculiar grin on his lips.

'I'll be damned, it is you. I thought you were dead.'

Trace remained silent, loathing on his face and death in his eyes. He made a decision: he would not let Harrigan just shoot him. He would throw himself at the man. Although likely that would amount to suicide, he would do his damnedest to take the hardcase to hell with him.

'You ain't afraid of me, are you, McCoy? You been chasin' me all these years and I ain't even known it. Reckon shootin's too good for the likes of that.' Harrigan suddenly threw the gun across the deck and Trace couldn't have been more shocked if the pirate had blown his own brains out. In nearly the same motion, the outlaw plucked the cutlass from its sheath and swung it up in front of Trace.

'You know what pirates did with traitors, McCoy? They made 'em walk the plank, way I'm gonna make you.'

What the hell was the man up to? The moat couldn't be more than ten feet across and the plank maybe ten feet above the water. The drop wasn't enough to kill and any man capable of swimming would make it across easily. Harrigan had some other reason for wanting Trace in that water. The glimpse of that dark shape rose in his mind and he wagered that had something to do with it. Something lay beneath that water, something deadly. Trace had no idea what but he wasn't about to accommodate the gang leader and find out.

Harrigan must have sensed a move coming because he suddenly jabbed the tip of the sword into Trace's shoulder. A spike of pain radiated across his chest and he gripped the wound. It wasn't deep but it hurt like hell and blood streamed down his chest.

Harrigan flashed the blade in a short arc that would have taken his head off his shoulders if he hadn't dived sideways in time. The outlaw's booming laugh shuddered through the air and one of the girls let out a chopped scream.

Trace slammed sideways against the rail, grabbing the beam and trying to whirl before Harrigan came at him with another blow, but was too late. The cutlass arched down and Trace stumbled right, barely avoiding its rapier edge. It cleaved a chunk of wood from the rail. Harrigan, obviously highly skilled with the weapon, yanked the blade free and jabbed at Trace's belly.

McCoy stumbled backward, but the pirate leader stepped in, jabbing with the blade. Trace scrambled sideways, without realizing it, ending up backed against the rail opening. Harrigan had deftly maneuvered him to the plank and swept the cutlass back and forth to prevent McCoy from diving to either side.

Harrigan inched forward, thrusting the sword before him. Trace had nowhere else to go; he stepped backward on to the plank but his balance was off and his boot slipped over the edge. He found himself suddenly going downward. A scream came from one of the girls.

He made a desperate grab, managing to wrap his right arm around the plank. He clung to it, suspended over the water, wounded left arm dangling at his side. He had little strength remaining in that arm, and what was there was fading rapidly.

Harrigan came on to the plank and peered down at him. Trace saw his own death staring back from the man's eye.

'You damn sure won't be comin' back after me this time, McCoy. Say hi to that gal of yours after you die. She was barely worth my time.' The pirate leader jerked the blade up and Trace knew when it descended it would sever his arm from his shoulder.

The cutlass streaked downward in a flash of silver. Trace refused to avert his eyes from Harrigan. He would show no fear; he refused to give the sonofabitch that satisfaction.

A gunshot cracked through the canyon and the pirate leader jerked, the blade jumping from his hand and sailing downward past Trace's face. It splashed into the water, disappearing. Some sort of commotion arose from beneath the surface but he had no chance to glimpse what caused it. His gaze swung to the ground, where Coralie stood with the derringer held straight-armed, clutched in white hands. The bullet had opened a gory streak across the pirate leader's inner forearm. Trace reckoned she had aimed at the outlaw's chest and missed, but the shot had saved his life none the less.

She triggered a second shot but the bullet went far wide.

Harrigan let out a roar. The first shot had thrown him off balance and he stumbled on the plank. Regaining his footing, he started to bring a heel down on Trace's arm.

McCoy's left hand shot out in a last desperate attempt, grabbing for the man's ankle. He jerked, the effort carrying little strength, but just enough.

Harrigan, looking down with a panicked expression, tried to pull his ankle loose. Trace's fingers dug into the boot, struggled to hold on.

The gang leader gave another tremendous jerk. Trace let go at the same instant. Harrigan cursed and his arms windmilled as his foot swept from beneath him with enough force to throw his body forward. He pitched over the side, making a desperate grab at Trace on his way down. He missed, plunging headlong into the water with a great splash.

Trace struggled to pull himself up on to the plank. Arms trembling, he managed to sling a leg up and across the board and drag himself on to the deck.

Below, the water went deceptively quiet. Then it erupted in a great writhing mass of foam and thrashing tail. Dark leathery flesh twisted in furious motion and a huge angular head seemed to split in two, revealing rows of razor-sharp teeth. The cavernous gaping mouth clamped about the struggling figure of John Harrigan, who swung a hooked hand at the creature's scaled belly.

'Christamighty . . .' Trace whispered, sickened by the gruesome sight. The creature's jaws closed on the Harrigan's head. The pirate leader shrieked but the sound was snapped short. Trace turned away, unable to watch even Harrigan be taken in such a hideous manner. On the ground, Coralie stared, frozen, arms still straight out.

With a whipping of its enormous tail, the beast pulled the pirate leader beneath the water. A scarlet orchid blossomed across the surface.

Trace gained his feet, legs trembling and heart hammering. For five long years he had sought to put an end to John Harrigan and bring some small measure of justice to Karen's memory, but now that it was over he felt only a horrible sense of emptiness and lost chances.

He went to the girls and untied them. 'Your father sent me to get you back,' he told the young woman whom he recognized from the tintype. She began crying and another girl put an arm around her shoulders. He guided them down the rope bridge, each wary and trying not to look at the blood spreading across the water's surface.

Trace went to Coralie, who had lowered the gun.

'What . . . what was it?' A look of horror had frozen on her face.

Trace frowned. 'Some type of 'gator. Harrigan must have brought the damn thing here somehow, likely when it was smaller. Damn thing had to be fifteen feet if it was an inch.'

Coralie peered at the other girls and her lips began to tremble. 'There was a Chinese girl . . .'

One of the doves looked towards the water and shook her head and Coralie burst into tears. Trace took her in his arms and held her, knowing she would never get the image of her friend's horrible death out of her mind.

Two days later Trace, Coralie and Violet Chadburn approached the railroad man's office in Danton. They had stopped over in Lazarette to get Trace's arm fixed up and it would heal in time, though, in a sling now, he wouldn't have a lot of use in it for a few weeks.

They rode up to the office, dismounting, and Trace helped Violet from the saddle. The girl wasn't much of a rider and likely would be sore in the britches for a spell, but considering what she had gone through it wasn't much to tolerate. She had remained sullen for most of the trip.

Coralie hadn't spoken much, either. He knew she was dwelling on the death of her friend.

Trace's own thoughts had centered on Karen and his future now that the outlaw was dead. He had lost the need to continue manhunting; that desire died with Harrigan. An emptiness remained inside him, and likely it would never be gone but he knew a bullet to his head was no longer the answer. He would live with it and without hunting down hardcases. Karen would want that.

They stepped into the office and Rutherford Chadburn

looked up from behind his desk. As his gaze focused on his daughter, he sprang from his chair and rushed to her. She fell into his arms, tears streaking down her face, and Trace saw tears gloss the old man's eyes as well.

'Thank you, Mr McCoy. Thank you for bringing my daughter back to me.'

Trace nodded. 'The man who took her won't trouble no one any more.'

'Why, Mr McCoy? Why did he take her?'

'Harrigan trafficked in women. Sold them as wives or slaves. I reckon there's no tellin' how many gals he done it to, but I'll turn the Pinkertons on to it. If there's a chance at finding any of them, they will.'

'I have a last favor to ask of you, Mr McCoy. There's a draft in the amount of five thousand dollars in my desk and a home in Denver for gals who ain't been as lucky growing up as Violet. The draft is made out in your name. I'd be right honored if you'd deliver it.'

'Reckon I'm the one who'd be honored, Mr Chadburn.'

The older man smiled a thin smile, still holding his daughter. 'Railroad owns a lot of land, Mr McCoy. I got a few hundred acres sitting north of here just doin' nothing. I could have the title drawn up by the time you get back, if you're inclined to settle down.'

'He'll take it,' Coralie suddenly put in. She glanced at him, then the old man. Trace looked at Chadburn and nodded. Maybe that was the best thing for him.

Coralie gave a thin smile then walked outside. Trace tipped his hat to the old man and looked at his daughter, who whispered a teary-eyed, 'Thank you.'

'What will you do now, ma'am?'

She looked at her father. 'I'm going back to Mississippi to get married, Mr McCoy.'

'With a couple armed guards this time,' Chadburn added.

Trace uttered a small laugh and left the office, his soul heavy. He now would have a tract of land, something he and Karen had always dreamed about but she wouldn't be there to share it with him. Her memory would, always, and that would have to do.

Sighing, he looked at the horses, but saw Coralie nowhere in sight. He stepped from the boardwalk and came around the mounts, searching the street. He spotted her stepping into the saloon where Harrigan had taken so much from her that fateful night.

Crossing the street, he came up behind her just inside the batwings. The place had wasted no time reopening, a new man behind the counter, but the tell-tale signs of that night's events remained in evidence.

Coralie stood peering into the barroom, wrapping her arms about herself, a distant look on her face.

'This where you want to be?' He asked it tentatively, afraid she would answer yes.

She turned and looked at him, tears in her eyes. 'No, Mr McCoy. I'm sayin' goodbye to what used to be my life.'

'You asked me a bit ago what lay beyond killing Harrigan for me.' His gaze held hers and she remained silent, perhaps a glint of hope in her eyes. 'Reckon I still don't know. Maybe I'll never know till I'm lookin' back.'

'Until then, Mr McCoy?' Her voice came out a whisper.

'Until then I need someone to show me it ain't just an empty trail.'

He took her hand and led her outside. For the first time in five years Trace McCoy was a man without a mission . . .

Unless it was just plain living.